LiKE BLOOD iN WATER

LIKE BLOOD IN WATER
YURIY TARNAWSKY

TUSCALOOSA

The University of Alabama Press
Tuscaloosa, Alabama 35487-0380

Published by FC2, an imprint of the University of Alabama Press, with
support provided by Florida State University and the Publications Unit of
the Department of English at Illinois State University

Address all editorial inquiries to: Fiction Collective Two, Florida State
University, c/o English Department, Tallahassee, FL 32306-1580

⊗

The paper on which this book is printed meets the minimum requirements
of American National Standard for Information Sciences—Permanence of
Paper for Printed Library Materials, ANSI Z39.48–1984

Library of Congress Cataloging-in-Publication Data
Tarnavskyi, IUrii.
    Like blood in water / by Yuriy Tarnawsky. — 1st ed.
        p. cm.
    ISBN-13: 978-1-57366-135-5 (pbk. : alk. paper)
    ISBN-10: 1-57366-135-X (pbk. : alk. paper)
    I. Title.
    PS3570.A64L55 2007
    813'.54—dc22
                                            2006029456

Cover Design: Lou Robinson
Book Design: Jennifer Pliler and Tara Reeser
Typeface: Garamond
Produced and printed in the United States of America

To the memory of my parents,
Olha and Ivan Tarnawsky—
these memories of my childhood

LiKE BLOOD iN WATER
FiVE MiNiNOVELS

contents

SCREAMING

1. the church

As Roark crossed the street and continued walking along the sidewalk, in this block flanked on the right by a tall iron fence overgrown with ivy, he heard a loud noise coming from the building on the other side and immediately labeled it as the scream of a large group of people united in an uncontrolled, limitless feeling of despair. Intrigued, his heart beating with excitement, he stopped without turning his head in the direction of the building, his ear cocked so that it could best catch the sounds coming from it, and listened. The noise lasted another six or seven seconds, abruptly stopped, and then started up again to last about the same amount of time, in other words some ten seconds.

Even while keeping his head straight while listening, by shifting his eyes right, Roark saw that the building the noise was coming from was a church and when silence followed the third wave of screaming he turned his head right and saw the top of the tall brown stone walls punctuated at regular intervals by the narrow ogival arches of the windows, the gray slate roof reaching desperately upward, and the small, rudimentary spires, undeveloped like limbs of thalidomide babies, on the background of the darkening evening sky, the color of brown-tinted car window glass.

He recalled then he had seen the facade of the church as he was crossing the street—it was readily visible from that side, since the fence in front of it was much shorter than on the side—but had not paid any attention to it, being absorbed in his thoughts. He had not seen the church before, having never been in that part of town.

An uncontrollable urge whose nature was unknown to him, like an invisible thread, jerked him and he quickly turned around, walked back to the corner of the street he had just crossed, turned left, and headed toward the gate in the fence opposite the main door of the church. He had to see what was going on inside.

The screaming resumed as Roark closed the front gate and was walking toward the church and he quickened his step, afraid it would stop before he had a chance to get inside. The door was wide and tall, appropriately bright red like a badly inflamed throat, and to Roark's relief opened obligingly before him; he had been afraid it would be locked.

The first scream ended and the second one began when Roark entered the church. It was brightly lit, so that Roark had to squint, and he realized he hadn't seen the light from the outside because the windows in the church were all boarded up. The church was also stripped bare of all religious trappings, its space completely empty. Roark remembered then he hadn't seen any crosses on the outside of the church—the facade or the roof—which had surprised him although he hadn't become aware of it at the time. The building had obviously been acquired by some secular entity and was used for non-religious purposes.

Before him, stretched out on their backs on the floor, each on his/her own mat of the type used by the yoga crowd, lay some fifty to sixty people, their heads turned toward the wall against which the altar once stood and their feet toward him. They were arranged more or less in rows, but in front of them, like the leader of a band or a military formation, lay a man, clearly the lead person of the group. The scream filled the vast space of the church, stopped for a brief period, and then was repeated for the third time. No direction came from the man in front—the group was obviously adept at what it was doing.

The screaming then stopped and everyone got up as if on command. The session was over. The man in charge was dressed in a pair of overalls soiled with brown dirt, and the same kind of dirt was visible on his hands and face, especially the forehead. Next to the man's mat on the floor lay a big shovel, its tip likewise caked with dirt, which the man picked up as he was getting ready to leave. All of this made Roark think of a gravedigger and he was puzzled. Did the man rush in straight from his gravedigger's job and have no time to change? But then why the shovel? At the same time Roark tried to figure out what the group was. He remembered hearing about a school of therapy called "the primal scream." Was this what the group was practicing? But he hadn't heard about that approach for years and thought it had gone out of style. He didn't know what to think.

2. a conversation

Just then a woman detached herself from the group and came up to Roark. She had lain in the center, a few rows in, was middle-aged, short, heavy, missing her left arm, and had a white string tied diagonally across her pasty, fat face. It had cut itself into her flesh like into a soft package, pushing it out of shape. She was dressed in an old, faded, navy blue sweat suit with the left sleeve tucked inside it. The following conversation took place between her and Roark.

Woman (*looking up at Roark since he is much taller, her head tilted to one side, the weight of her body shifted onto that foot and her voice brimming with goodwill and curiosity*): Have you been coming here long?

Roark (*not in the least startled*): No, it's my first time here.

Woman (*pushing on, as if not caring about the answer*): Did you enjoy the screaming?

Roark: Oh, yes. I was enthused by it. It really had meaning for me. It projected good energy.

Woman (*tilting her head the other way and shifting the weight of her body onto the other foot*): Have you ever screamed?

Roark (*understands what she means*): No, but I plan to.

Woman: Roger'll sign you up. Talk to him. (*Without a pause.*) What's your name?

Roark: Rilke.

Woman (*visibly intrigued, tilting her head and shifting her weight to the other side again*): Rilke? That's wonderful. What's your first name?

Roark: Rilke's my first name. My last name is Roark.

Woman: Oh, what an interesting name...both of them.... (*Without a pause again.*) Were your parents crazy about Rilke? Like, was he their favorite poet?

Roark: My father was fond of him. He came from Switzerland, the place where Rilke died...Val-Mont. (*Without a pause in turn, copying the woman.*) What's YOUR name?

Woman (*quickly*): Alba.

Roark: Alma? That's wonderful. It means "soul" in Spanish.

Woman: No, Alba...for the Duchess of Alba that Goya painted. My father came from Spain, the place where Goya was born...Fuendetodos. (*Without a pause again.*) I didn't know

Alma means "soul" in Spanish. My father didn't teach me the language.

Roark (*giving up on the topic, eager to get to what interests him*): Is Roger a gravedigger?

Woman (*turning her head around for an instant and looking at the leader who is just disappearing in one of the doors*): No, he's a stockbroker.

Roark (*incredulous*): A stock broker?... Really? Why is he all covered with dirt and why does he have that shovel?

Woman (*laughing*): Oh, that's for screaming. It helps you to scream better when you have the right objects near you. (*Without a pause, as so many times before.*) Do you know what I use to help me scream?

Roark: No.

Woman (*beaming with joy*): A fetus! (*Turning away from Roark.*) I'll show you....

She runs to her mat, picks up an object standing on the floor next to it, and in a few seconds is back with Roark. She shows him a glass jar filled with bluish liquid in which there floats a gray shape with ill-defined appendages like a botched poached egg. Roark looks at it with curiosity. He comes to the conclusion that the string tied over the woman's face is also a screaming aid. In the bright light the liquid in the jar sends off flashes like a beautiful blue eye.

3. rilke

Roark's dream.

Roark is walking up a garden path covered with sand. It crunches rhythmically under his feet. The ground slopes up— it is in Switzerland. Up ahead on the left grow bushes. Under one of them lies a human figure twisting on the ground. The person—it is a man—seems to be struggling with someone. Roark looks closer to see who the man's adversary is, but there isn't anyone there—the man is struggling with himself. And it isn't just a game—he is obviously desperate and seems to be fighting for his life.

Roark passes the man and sees the latter is dressed in a tight-fitting black suit and has a well-formed head with black, closely cropped hair and a trimmed beard. He realizes it is Rilke. He doesn't dare to stop and look but walks on. It would be impolite to stare at someone in such a situation, especially a man of Rilke's stature.

Roark walks on and soon reaches the crest of the hill. It is actually the peak of a very tall mountain. It is craggy. Down below shimmers the sea. Ships and boats can be seen on it. The latter are mostly sailboats. Roark knows Geneva, which is in Switzerland, is on a lake, and in the dream the lake has turned into a sea. He is not aware of this discrepancy. He is elated by the sight and he stretches his arms out to the sides and fills his chest with air. It is fresh and invigorating. Roark laughs. Time to go back! Roark remembers Rilke under the bush. As he nears the spot he sees a black shape, all still, lying on the ground. Roark's heart beats faster. He is concerned something might have happened to Rilke. He is afraid he may have died. He rushes up to the bush and looks down. Rilke looks dead. He is like a suit thrown down on the ground in great haste. The phrase "irrelevant Rilke" passes through Roark's mind but he forgets it immediately. He worries about Rilke. The man is lying face down. Roark squats down beside him and turns him over. Rilke doesn't stir—he is definitely dead. His eyes are open and their irises have disappeared under his forehead. The sight is ghastly. Roark is frightened and disgusted at the same time. He quickly stands up, shooting up like a geyser. He then notices rose petals strewn all over the ground around Rilke. They are pink. The bush under which Rilke lies is a rosebush. It looks as if Rilke had struggled with the rosebush rather than himself and had lost. The rosebush has killed him. Roark feels pain in his left hand. He opens it and looks. There is a wound in it like in Christ's hand after he was taken off the cross. Blood flows from it. Roark then realizes he is clutching something in his right hand. He wants to see what it is and looks at it. It is a dagger. It is old-fashioned, with an ornate handle and a rhomboid blade. He doesn't know what to do with it.

Alba's dream.

Alba is in her kitchen, cooking. There is a big old-fashioned stove there, pots and pans are all around, and the windows are high up under the ceiling and are small. It seems to be in a basement of an old house—the walls are very thick. The air is full of steam and the smell of cooking. It is not pleasant. Then a tall male figure, all in black, comes into the kitchen. It is Rilke. He comes up to the stove, stands next to Alba, and starts stirring in the pot in front of him. Alba looks into the pot and sees it is full of little round gray things in a broth or thin sauce.

They're fetuses. Rilke is cooking a fetus stew! Alba is aghast—
who would eat it?! She can't believe Rilke would do anything
like that. He stirs the stew vigorously however. He then turns
to her and says it won't be enough. Alba forgets about her aver-
sion and agrees with Rilke there won't be enough stew. What
are they to do? Rilke suggests they chop off his left arm and
add it to the stew. Alba sees no other solution. He says for her
to help him get out of his clothes. She unbuttons his tight jacket and takes it off. Then they jointly take off his shirt. She still
has two arms like she used to. A long serrated knife finds itself
in Alba's hand. She starts sawing away with it at Rilke's arm at
the shoulder. Rilke doesn't protest in any way. He docsn't seem
to feel any pain. Alba saws through his flesh. She hits the bone.
It shows in the wound. It is white and shines like mother-of-
pearl. Alba can see the bone move in the joint.

4. the apartment

Following is a description of Roark and Alba's
apartment after they got married.

It is one very large room in a former factory building with windows along the entire outside wall. In the middle of it stands
a toilet bowl without a seat. An old black quilt lies in a heap
next to it. You can cover yourself with it when you use the
toilet if you so desire. A large, old-fashioned sink with two
basins is attached in the center of the wall opposite to the
one with the windows. It is used for washing up as well as for
doing dishes. On the left of it stands a refrigerator and on the
right a gas stove. Both are old and white. On the right side
of the stove stand two gray industrial-style metal cupboards

used for storing dishes, food, and clothes. In the corner of the room beyond the metal cupboards, at an angle of forty-five degrees, stands a large red tent which serves as the bedroom. It is chock-full of pillows, quilts, sleeping bags, and other bed clothing. Mingled in among them is an old-fashioned black rotary telephone. A wire is stretched above the tent from one wall to the next on which there hang clothes, both on hangers and merely draped over. In the opposite corner, also at an angle of forty-five degrees, that is, like a mirror image of the tent, stands a cube, about six feet on each side, with old, rusty pipes forming each of its twelve edges. It is called "the screaming cube" and screaming sessions are conducted in it. On the wall next to it, attached with scotch tape, hangs a full-size, high-quality reproduction of Edvard Munch's famous lithograph *The Scream*. In the very corner behind the cube stands a beautiful old grandfather clock, an heirloom from Roark's family, built by Roark's paternal grandfather upon the completion of his apprenticeship and admission to the rank of master clockmaker in Switzerland. A roughly twenty-foot long wooden industrial workbench, badly beaten up and stained with oil in places, stands in the middle of the room. It serves as a table. Piled up on it are dishes, kitchen utensils, books, papers, toilet articles, clothes, and so on. There are no chairs next to it nor anywhere else in the apartment. Four very bright fluorescent lamps arranged in a row high up on the ceiling illuminate the room. The walls in the room are painted white. The paint is old and peels in places. The floor is wooden, badly scuffed up, and stained with oil in places like the table.

The windowsills are all taken up with flowerpots, empty bottles, figurines of various sorts, and so on. On one of them stand glass jars containing fetuses. There are seven of them, three with the liquid tinged pink and four blue, for female and male, respectively. The windows have rusty metal frames, the color of dried blood. Their small panes are dusty. Outside stretches a monotonous urban landscape of single-storied buildings with flat roofs, a smoggy sky above them.

5. screaming

Roark and Alba are sitting in the screaming cube in a position similar to the lotus position, looking each other in the eyes and screaming. This is an advanced position, used only by expert screamers. The screaming has nothing to do with either "primal scream" therapy or the practice of shattering glass for show-off purposes which so fascinated Lorca and Günther Grass. Rather, its foundation lies in the writings—a single article in German of a couple dozen pages titled *"Zur Theorie und Praxis des Geschreis,"* that is, "Toward a Theory and Practice of Screaming"—by the obscure late nineteenth-century Austrian mystic and inventor of Ruthenian background K. Ryk. It maintains that screaming, when performed properly, may have profound effects on the surroundings as well as the very person of the screamer with metaphysical consequences.

The combined scream of Roark and Alba is truly ear-shattering, reminiscent of the wailing of a siren, but also calming like an ostinato note in a musical composition, for instance one of Bach's keyboard pieces played on the organ. Because of its first quality one would expect that the neighbors above, below, and on both sides of Roark and Alba's apartment would react to the screaming by knocking on the floor, ceiling, or walls in indignation. This is not true however because all of Roark and Alba's neighbors have moved out a long time ago, unable to prevent the couple from exercising their rights to self-expression. It is for the same reason the owners of the building—a partnership of a few Japanese individuals—have not been able to evict them.

As the screaming goes on, a sound comes out of the mouth of the figure in Munch's lithograph—at first faint and hesitant, at times stopping altogether, but gradually growing louder and louder, more and more sure of itself, until finally uniting with the screams of Roark and Alba into one, as strong and as confident as they, perfectly matched with them as the third voice in a perfectly matched trio of singers, the united scream conveying a boundless feeling of despair that lies at its core as the sound of a perfectly matched trio of singers conveys the beauty that lies at the core of its singing, continuing unchanged from then on, powerful, steady, with no end in sight. The hands of the grandfather clock tremble, hesitate, stop, then move back in short, tentative movements, until finally they spin madly in the counterclockwise direction. A red and blue light, like vapor, appears in the room, growing denser and denser with time, coalescing toward the center, until it forms a bright pink ball that settles over the toilet bowl, hiding it completely. The fetuses in the jar stir shyly, then move more and more boldly, spinning and tumbling, swimming as much as they are able in their cramped spaces, looking like a team of world class athletes in the sport of synchronized underwater swimming recently admitted to the Olympics.

6. the final scene

It is evening, early spring. Roark is standing on the bank of a huge river, his back turned to the world. On the other side the sun is setting. There is no one around. Roark is screaming. The river is high, its banks overflowing with the spring flood. It flows right to left, fast, almost like a train moving, carrying huge floats of ice together with objects of various types on them, such as houses, barns, sheds, outhouses, trucks, cars, farm machinery, furniture, bedding, household articles, and so on. For some reason among the latter there appear very frequently grandfather clocks which are usually standing up. Occasionally a solitary human figure can be seen floating by—a middle-aged woman standing at the edge of a float, staring blank-eyed into distance, as if through a window, a young man lying face down, his head cradled in his hands, an old man frozen still in his rocking chair.

The earth is flat and perfectly bare, without a trace of plant life on it. It is a rich brown however, and looks fluffy, so it is probably very fertile and will eventually sprout lush vegetation. Apparently it has been a very hard winter until recently. The sky above is also brown, tinged by the light reflecting from below. It is very low—so low Roark has to stand with his head bent down. It stretches flat all the way to the horizon where there is only a thin opening left between it and the earth like the slot in a pinball machine. Someone on the other side is feeding shiny new quarters of light into it one by one, over and over again.

FORMER PIANIST FITIPALDO

1. prologue

Former pianist Nelson Fitipaldo stood at his kitchen window and looked outside. It was actually his whole apartment—what was left of his modest four-room, kitchen, and bathroom place after he sold the four rooms and the bathroom to his neighbor from across the wall, Rodrigo Vargas, which the latter annexed to his modest four room, kitchen, and bathroom apartment, turning it into a spacious habitat.

The window in the kitchen ran the length of the wall; the building was once a factory and had been converted into condominiums. Its iron frame was badly rusted and imparted this quality to the image of the world outside. The kitchen-apartment was on the third floor and afforded a good view of the landscape stretching away to the horizon. Right under the window was a narrow strip of asphalt which served as the access road to the car garages some people in the building owned. (Nelson Fitipaldo was not one of them.) It was wide enough for a small car to be parked in it while permitting other cars to travel back and forth and at this time two such vehicles were huddling with their passenger sides against the rusty, partly fallen down chain-link fence that ran along the property line, their front sides pointing left. On the other side of the chain-link fence lay an athletic field, one of a few such in town. It consisted of a soccer field, a cinder track around it, and an area for other sports activities such as long and high jump, shot put, and gymnastics. The gymnastic equipment was a high bar, parallel bars, and rings. In one corner of this area there were set up a few swings for children of spectators and sports participants to play on while the latter were busy, respectively watching or exercising.

On the other side of the athletic field stretched the edge of the town with its single-storied, mostly flat-roofed houses that looked like garbage strewn haphazardly over the flat land. Laundry hung out to dry on clotheslines could be seen here and there among them. On one such line was pinned a small rectangle of the worn, faded blue, percale sky. It fluttered in the strong breeze.

The town—Fim do Mundo or End of the World—being on the Mato Grosso plateau, was close to the sky and the goal on the right side of the soccer field was so close to the horizon that its net was pushed in at one corner in the back. There was a game in progress on the soccer field and the players, tiny, the size of wooden figurines on a Christmas tree, dressed in black and white and red and white, were running frantically all over the field like ants in an anthill somebody had stepped into. The ball was nowhere to be seen and they were desperately trying to find it.

An athlete, as it appeared, a man, ran down the long jump path, obviously straining to the limit but in reality moving as slowly as a sloth. When he took off into the air the sand pit before him exploded forward and became as long as a runway capable of accommodating supersonic aircraft. It ended at the horizon. There was no telling how much longer it might have extended if it didn't have to stop there. The athlete was left suspended in the air, waiting for a parachute to help him come down.

2. what nelson fitipaldo's apartment looked like

As was said, Nelson Fitipaldo's apartment was a kitchen. It was long and narrow—some thirty feet by about seven. The long wall was all a window. It faced south. Because the window was so large and the apartment so narrow the latter was very bright. The light in it was stacked like new wooden boards floor to ceiling. This was especially true along the back wall.

The kitchen sink and the stove in the apartment stood against the back wall. The sink was long and narrow, of the industrial type, being left over from when the building was a factory. It was divided into two basins.

There was no bathroom in the apartment. As was also said, it had been sold with the four rooms. To wash up, one had to use the kitchen sink. One could stand in it to take a sponge bath. To relieve oneself, one had to use a chamber pot. Nelson Fitipaldo emptied it into the drain in the street usually in the middle of the night when there was no one around.

The apartment was sparsely furnished. It had a table, two chairs, and two cupboards. The table stood in the middle of the apartment. It was a hospital operating table. The chairs stood at the opposite narrow ends of the table. They were old-fashioned dentist's chairs and were fastened to the floor. The cupboards were of metal, the industrial type. The table also served as a bed. Going to sleep, Nelson Fitipaldo would put a thin mattress, a pillow, and bed linen on it, which he kept rolled up in one of the cupboards. During the daytime he sometimes took naps in one of the dentist's chairs. For some reason he preferred the one closer to the door although they were both identical. He never dreamed about being operated on while sleeping on the table nor about having a toothache while napping in the chair.

3. how nelson fitipaldo sold his apartment

There is a knock on Nelson Fitipaldo's apartment door. Nelson Fitipaldo opens it and sees his neighbor from across the wall, Rodrigo Vargas, standing with an expression of big surprise on his face.

Rodrigo Vargas (*the surprise on his face turning into a decal*): What are you doing here, Dom Nelson?

Nelson Fitipaldo: I live here.

Rodrigo Vargas (*a decal of anger replacing the decal of surprise*): How can you live here, when I live here?

Nelson Fitipaldo (*calmly and extremely politely*): This cannot be, Dom Rodrigo. I have lived here fourteen years, seven months, five hours and…(*He looks at his watch.*) thirty-seven minutes.

Rodrigo Vargas (*the decal of anger turning red and becoming three-dimensional*): Don't act like a clown, Dom Nelson! This is my place! Get out of my way! (*He forces his way into the apartment.*)

Nelson Fitipaldo obediently steps aside and lets Rodrigo Vargas come into the hallway.

Nelson Fitipaldo (*most gently and politely*): You are welcome to come in Dom Rodrigo. See for yourself.

Rodrigo Vargas steps into the apartment and sees his mistake.

Rodrigo Vargas (*seeing his mistake, but with no trace of guilt*): You're right, Dom Nelson. This is your apartment…or at least it's not mine. I took the garbage out without taking my keys with me and accidentally knocked on your door instead of mine. My mistake.

Nelson Fitipaldo (*very politely*): It's understandable, Dom Rodrigo. It can happen to anyone.

Rodrigo Vargas does not listen to Nelson Fitipaldo. He walks around him and continues into the apartment. Nelson Fitipaldo follows him.

Rodrigo Vargas (*while walking*): It's a nice place you have here... just like mine.

Nelson Fitipaldo (*following closely behind Rodrigo Vargas*): Yes it is. They're all the same.

Rodrigo Vargas (*examining each of the four rooms, kitchen, and bathroom, and summing up in the end*): Two bedrooms, living room, dining room, kitchen, and bathroom.

Nelson Fitipaldo: That's right.

Rodrigo Vargas (*stopping suddenly, turning around to face Nelson Fitipaldo and projecting contempt*): Do you need all this space?

Nelson Fitipaldo is put on the spot. He can of course use all the space but isn't sure he has to. He doesn't know how to answer.

Rodrigo Vargas (*seizing the moment, forcefully, while pointing at the room next to which they are standing*): Sell me this room.

Nelson Fitipaldo (*hesitates, but then gives in*): All right.

Rodrigo Vargas looks around, walks to the door of the next room, and stops.

Rodrigo Vargas: And how about this one?

Nelson Fitipaldo (*hesitates a shade longer*): You can have this one too, Dom Rodrigo.

Emboldened by easy success Rodrigo Vargas turns away from Nelson Fitipaldo and walks down the hallway, looking again into the other rooms. Nelson Fitipaldo follows him with a somewhat worried face. It is almost certain he doesn't know what the cause of it is however. Rodrigo Vargas checks out the rest of the apartment and turns around to face Nelson Fitipaldo.

Rodrigo Vargas: Sell me the other two rooms, Dom Nelson, and the bathroom. You can have the kitchen. It's big. You'll have plenty of space.

Nelson Fitipaldo hesitates. Two seconds go by. Rodrigo Vargas decides to act.

Rodrigo Vargas (*derisively*): I see you're hesitating, Dom Nelson. What's the matter? You can't part with those rooms?

Nelson Fitipaldo (*embarrassed, turning red*): No, no, Dom Rodrigo, you can...I mean, I can part with them.... You can have the two...I mean four rooms...and the bathroom.... I don't need them....

Rodrigo Vargas (*feeling the victor and proud of it*): Wonderful! It's a deal. (*He offers Nelson Fitipaldo his hand.*) Let's shake hands on it.

Nelson Fitipaldo obediently extends his hand to Rodrigo Vargas. They shake hands. Rodrigo Vargas slaps Nelson Fitipaldo on the back. This makes Nelson Fitipaldo feel great. The incertitude of how to feel vanishes from Nelson Fitipaldo's face and is replaced by an expression of relief. It isn't a decal however. Nelson Fitipaldo is not a person of the decal-expression type. Rodrigo Vargas takes another walk down the hallway, looking into all the rooms that are soon to be his, is satisfied with what he sees, walks to the outside door with Nelson Fitipaldo behind him, opens the door, and turns once more to Nelson Fitipaldo.

Rodrigo Vargas: I will check on the current prices at city hall and have my notary get in touch with you.

Nelson Fitipaldo is pleased to hear this.

Nelson Fitipaldo (*bowing just a little*): Thank you, Dom Rodrigo.

Rodrigo Vargas (*remembering at the last moment*): Do you have a notary?

Nelson Fitipaldo (*taken aback, feeling guilty*): Nnooo.... I don't....

Rodrigo Vargas (*reassuring*): That's all right. My notary will find you one. They'll come together.

Nelson Fitipaldo (*very obliged, bowing more pronouncedly*): Thank you, Dom Rodrigo, thank you.

Rodrigo Vargas (*stepping outside*): Don't mention it, Dom Nelson. Good-bye. (*In the corridor.*) See you soon.

Nelson Fitipaldo (*still bowing*): See you soon, Dom Rodrigo.... Yes.... Good-bye. Thank you.

There is no response from Rodrigo Vargas. He disappears from Nelson Fitipaldo's sight. Nelson Fitipaldo shuts the door. As if he had been impatiently waiting for an opportunity to do this, he quickly turns around, walks to his kitchen, stands at the window, and looks outside.

4. how nelson fitipaldo stopped playing the piano

It happened during a recital, when Nelson Fitipaldo was in his forties, at the peak of his admittedly not brilliant but respectable career. Actually the process started during the rehearsal sessions before the recital although the real end came when Nelson Fitipaldo was performing on the stage.

The first sign of what was going to happen was that in the middle of a rehearsal session a week before the concert Nelson Fitipaldo suddenly stopped playing with his right hand. He had a feeling it wasn't there. So his left hand went on playing but the right one wouldn't. A deep fear seized Nelson Fitipaldo. He couldn't understand what had happened to his right hand. He glanced at it, and it was there, with its fingers on the keyboard, except they weren't moving. The hand wasn't limp, nor did he lose sensation in it, for it was firm and he could feel the smoothness and cold of the keys under his fingers, but it refused to move. It seemed to be convinced it wasn't there. Nelson Fitipaldo thought this would last forever but his seeing his hand seemed to bring life back into it and all of a sudden it started playing again, at a point where it should have. Nelson Fitipaldo was shaken by the incident, but it was over and his hand went on playing as if it had never stopped, and so he let his attention be sucked in by the vortex of the music and forgot about what had happened. Within a matter of seconds it was as if it had never taken place.

The next few rehearsals went without a hitch and Nelson Fitipaldo would have forgotten the first incident for good but then, unexpectedly, in the middle of another rehearsal a few days before the recital the same thing happened. The piece Nelson Fitipaldo was playing wasn't the same, so his stopping had nothing to do with the music, but suddenly his right hand again stopped playing, seeming not to be there. Nelson Fitipaldo remembered then the previous incident (this time it was as if he had never forgotten it) and was again seized by a deep fear that was even stronger than the first one—the frightening thing had happened a second time! Nelson Fitipaldo glanced at his right hand and there it was resting on the keyboard as the first time, convinced it wasn't there. His left hand went on playing, and this time his right hand hesitated just a shade longer, but then it did start up playing as before, in the spot it was supposed to. Nelson Fitipaldo dwelt on the incident a little longer this time but the music again absorbed his attention and he forgot about what had happened. The remaining couple of rehearsals before the performance again went without a hitch and when Nelson Fitipaldo went out onto the stage for his recital there was no trace of fear in him. The memory of the two incidents seemed to have been pushed permanently out of his mind.

It was an all-Chopin concert and the first half went perfectly. But during the second half, in the middle of the Grand Polonaise, Nelson Fitipaldo's right hand stopped playing again and he instantly recalled the previous two incidents as if they had happened just seconds before this one. He felt that things wouldn't go as well this time as on the previous two occasions and his stomach was one big cramp like the clenched fist of a giant man that had somehow found its way inside him. Nelson Fitipaldo glanced at his right hand and saw it resting on the keyboard in the now familiar fashion. His heart was up in his throat throbbing wildly and his shirt collar was choking him. He visualized his hand starting to play as it had done twice before when he looked at it but this time nothing happened. The hand remained still, convinced it wasn't there. His left hand then stopped playing. It seemed to feel there was no point in continuing alone. Sweat ran down his forehead and collected in a drop on the tip of his nose. Quickly he stuck his right hand in his breast pocket, got out the handkerchief he kept there for such occasions, wiped his face with it, stuck it back in the pocket, and then brought both his hands down in despair on the keyboard. His left hand started playing immediately but his right one refused. It simply wasn't there! He looked at it again and this time knew there was no use. His hand would never play again. He stopped playing with his left hand and got up from the bench. His shirt stuck to his back under his jacket and he wished he could move away from it as from a disgustingly sweaty body that had pressed itself unceremoniously against his. He became aware then of the large arrangement of white flowers stacked in tiers next to the curtain on the other side of the piano. He had noticed it before but had forgotten about it, being absorbed in the music. Now it reminded him of funerals.

It was a fitting end to his career as a pianist. For some reason this made him feel better. He turned right and walked out from behind the bench. The hall was a huge black hole before him, with no one in it. He bowed toward it (it naturally didn't respond) and walked off the stage.

5. flower dream no. 1

Nelson Fitipaldo dreams he walks out onto a stage, very fast, as if in a hurry to get to the other side, for instance to catch a train that is about to leave. A wall of white flowers arranged in tiers is blocking his way however. They stand along where the curtain on the other side of the stage should be, reaching higher than he is tall. Empty space, brightly lit, can be seen behind them. Nelson Fitipaldo doesn't see the flowers at first so that when he finally does they are right in front of him and he has to stop abruptly, getting up on his toes and leaning forward, carried by the momentum. He manages to hold himself back so that he doesn't fall over onto the flowers however. A hand then appears suddenly from among the flowers and grabs his. It is someone's right hand and it grabs his left. The hand is white, bony, ice-cold, and very strong. Nelson Fitipaldo is horrified by the hand and tries to free himself from its grip by pulling his hand away and stepping back. The hand is like a vise however and doesn't let him go. It pulls him forward steadily among the flowers and in the end he falls into them headfirst as if into water.

Right on the other side of the wall of flowers there stands a long and tall rectangular table such as you see in operating rooms in a hospital or a morgue, and a tall, thin male figure lies

on it face up. It is this person's hand that has pulled Nelson
Fitipaldo into the room and is gripping his. Nelson Fitipaldo
looks at the man. He is a total stranger, with a chalk-white face
and long black hair, slicked back, and is dressed in a black suit
with the same color tie and white shirt. He lies completely still
and stiff, as if dead, but his eyes and lips are tightly pressed
together, forming wrinkles, as in people trying to suppress
laughter.

This terrifies Nelson Fitipaldo even more and he tries again to
free himself from the man's grip but the harder he tries, the
stronger the man holds him. He feels in the end the man is
going to crush his hand. It hurts so much he finally has to stop
trying to get away.

He looks at the man's face again. The wrinkles around his
eyes and mouth have gotten even more pronounced and they
shake. The man is clearly trying to stop himself from bursting
out with laughter. His right eye then, the one closer to Nelson
Fitipaldo, opens up a little and, shiny and mischievous, looks
at Nelson Fitipaldo. It winks at him. The whole face then ex-
plodes in a burst of laughter so that Nelson Fitipaldo feels
the man's breath and even specks of saliva on his face. Taken
aback he doesn't know what to do, relaxes, and stops resisting the man. The latter then lifts his head off the table and,
still laughing, pulls Nelson Fitipaldo onto himself. Nelson Fitipaldo is horrified again and would like to get away but it is too
late. He falls onto the man as if into a deep hole. He screams
in terror and wakes up.

6. flower dream no. 2

Nelson Fitipaldo is walking at night. It is in the countryside, in Europe—Spain, Portugal, or Italy most probably. He is on the slope of a hill overgrown with soft grass. There is dew on the grass and it wets his feet—he is barefoot. The moon seems to be shining for he can see the countryside around him pretty well but he doesn't look at the sky to see the moon. To his right, in the valley, fog is rising or settling, mingling with the silvery, dewy grass. Nelson Fitipaldo is overcome with joy. He never felt so happy in his life. He thinks life is beautiful. He doesn't know where he is going but he is walking with a purpose. In fact he seems to be hurrying to get somewhere.

Finally he has come to the place of his destination. It is off the slope of the hill, at the edge of the valley. There is a small plot of ground there surrounded by an iron fence. There is a gate in the fence. Nelson Fitipaldo opens the gate and steps into the enclosure. He closes the gate. There is a large stone slab in the middle of the plot with the statue of a young woman at its farther narrow end under a huge, sheltering weeping willow tree. Nelson Fitipaldo notices he is carrying in his hand a bouquet of flowers—white lilies. He comes up to the stone slab and lays them down on it. The slab is marble. There is an inscription chiseled into it. Nelson Fitipaldo tries to read it but it is too dark for him to see. It seems to be a poem however and he can make out one word in it—"Laura." It is the name of the woman buried there. He has come to pay his respects to her memory. Nelson Fitipaldo isn't saddened by the realization a dead person dear to him lies under the stone slab. He is elated as before. The beauty of the world he is in permeates everything, even the notion of death. He wants to enjoy the surroundings. He sits down on the slab. Suddenly he feels something soft touch his shoulder. He thinks it is a branch of the willow tree. He looks and sees however a female figure sitting at his side. It is she who has touched him like a branch of the willow tree. Nelson Fitipaldo knows the woman—she is Laura, the person buried in the grave. He is not surprised she is at his side. He feels it is normal for dead people to come out of their graves. He has come to see her.

He knows the woman but doesn't know what she looks like. He looks at her. She is stunningly beautiful. Her hair is long and soft like the branches of the willow tree. She is extremely fair and her features are delicate, as if carved from marble. Her eyes are huge, with eyelashes like the petals of certain flowers, for instance daisies. Her irises are blue on the other hand like forget-me-nots.

Nelson Fitipaldo and the woman embrace. He feels the warmth and suppleness of her body. The latter reminds him again of the weeping willow branches with which they are surrounded. They kiss. Her hair envelops his face. It sticks to his skin. It gets between their lips. Nelson Fitipaldo has to disengage himself from the embrace and clear the woman's hair from his face. He has some difficulty in achieving the latter. He realizes it is because his face is all wet—he is crying. He is surprised at first because he feels so happy but then the fact seems normal to him—you don't have to be unhappy to cry. And yet his tears are not tears of joy. This bothers him. Then he realizes he is crying because the woman is dead. He feels he has to let her know this. He turns to her and says: "Laura, it's because you're dead!"

7. a theory of man
After Wittgenstein

Proposition.

0. man is

0.1 man is a body

0.1.1 a body perceives

0.1.1.1 a body perceives only what it can perceive

0.1.1.1.1 what a body does not perceive is not

0.1.1.2 a body that does not perceive is not

0.1.2 a body wants

0.1.2.1 a body wants only what it can want

0.1.2.1.1 a body can want what it cannot perceive

0.1.2.1.2 a body can want what it cannot think of

0.1.2.1.3 a body that does not want is not

0.1.3 a body thinks

0.1.3.1 a body thinks only what it can think of

0.1.3.1.1 a body can think only of what it can perceive

0.1.3.2 a body that does not think is not

0.1.4 a body feels

0.1.4.1 a body feels only what it can feel

0.1.4.1.1 a body can feel what it does not perceive

0.1.4.1.2 a body can feel what it does not think of

0.1.4.2 what a body feels is not the world

0.1.4.3 a body that does not feel is not

0.2 a body has beginning and end

Corollaries.

1. man is what his body is

1.1 man perceives

1.1.1 man perceives the world

1.1.1.1 the world is what man perceives

1.1.1.1.1 e.g., a line between two points is because man perceives it

1.1.1.1.2 e.g., a green world is because man perceives it

1.1.1.1.3 e.g., man is because man perceives himself

1.1.1.2 what man cannot perceive is not

1.1.1.2.1 e.g., fourth dimension is not because man cannot perceive it

1.1.1.2.2 e.g., a future world is not because man cannot perceive it

1.1.1.2.3 e.g., God is not because man cannot perceive him

1.2 man wants

1.2.1 man wants to be

1.2.1.1 man would not be if man did not want to be

1.2.1.1.1 man is because man is

1.2.1.1.1.1 man is his own cause

1.3 man thinks

1.3.1 man thinks of what may be

1.3.1.1 something may be because man can think of it

1.3.1.1.1 e.g., a future world may be because man can think of it

1.3.1.1.1.1 e.g., a rose-colored world may be because man can think of it

1.3.2 what may be may already be

1.3.2.1 e.g., the world that is that man thinks of already is

1.3.1 what man cannot think of may not be

1.3.1.1 e.g., a four-dimensional world may not be because man cannot think of it

1.3.1.1.1 therefore what man thinks of as a four-dimensional world is not a four-dimensional world

1.3.1.2 e.g., God may not be because man cannot think of him

1.3.1.2.1 therefore what man thinks of as God is not God

1.4 man feels

1.4.1 man feels what man cannot perceive

1.4.1.1 e.g., man feels sadness

1.4.1.2 e.g., man feels joy

1.4.1.3 e.g., man feels God

1.4.2 man feels what man cannot think of

1.4.2.1 e.g., man feels sadness

1.4.2.2 e.g., man feels joy

1.4.2.3 e.g., man feels God

1.4.3 what man feels is not the world

1.4.3.1 e.g., sadness is not the world

1.4.3.2 e.g., joy is not the world

1.4.3.3 e.g., God is not the world

Conclusions.

2. man will not be

2.1 man will not perceive

2.1.1 man will not perceive the world

2.1.1.1 the world will not be

2.1.1.1.1 e.g., lines between two points will not be

2.1.1.1.2 e.g., green worlds will not be

2.2 man will not want

2.2.1 man will not want to be

2.2.1.1 the cause for man's being will not be

2.3 man will not think

2.3.1 the world that is will not be

2.3.2 the world that may be will not be

2.3.2.1 e.g., future worlds may not be

2.3.2.1.1 e.g., rose-colored worlds may not be

2.4 man will not feel

2.4.1 e.g., sadness will not be felt

2.4.2 e.g., joy will not be felt

2.4.3 e.g., God will not be felt

8. last view of nelson fitipaldo's family

Nelson Fitipaldo's family—wife, daughter, and son—are going away for good. They are between Nelson Fitipaldo and the vanishing point on the horizon. His wife Lourdes goes first, leaning forward, her head bent down, protruding beyond her body, as if she were walking against a strong wind, but in reality protruding because of the vast space and emptiness before her and her determination to get away from her husband, a big suitcase in each of her hands, they seeming light, as though tending to rise like helium-filled balloons, as if wanting to ease her onerous task of getting away from her husband, the daughter Fatima behind her, her left hand clutching the skirt of her mother's overcoat, stretching it like a rubber membrane, stretching also her left arm as if it too were made from rubber, a two-dimensional object cut out of a rubber membrane, a smaller suitcase in her right hand, this one however heavy, not having a tendency to rise, the son Nelson II, the younger of the two children, also behind his mother, on her left, clutching the skirt of her overcoat with his right hand, stretching it more than his sister does and also much more his own arm so that it is blurred, seeming no longer to be made out of a rubber membrane but being a blur of an image projected at a sharp angle onto a surface so that it barely resembles a boy's arm, being rather a random mixture no longer even of forms but merely colors, a suitcase still smaller than his sister's in his left hand, this one also appearing heavy, not showing any tendency to rise, the boy also

a little behind his sister because of stretching his mother's coat
and his right arm more than she, undoubtedly because of being
younger and smaller and thus incapable of walking as fast, the
two children also leaning forward but not nearly as much as
their mother, partly because she is sheltering them from the
vast space and emptiness before them but also because they lack
their mother's determination to get away, merely following her
instinctively as children are apt to do with adults they are used
to obeying, this very likely being the reason for the children's
suitcases not showing any tendency to rise, they not having imparted it to the latter because of lacking their mother's determination to get away, all three bodies distorted, as if also made
out of rubber membranes that have been stretched, although
not as much as the arms of the two children, especially that of
the boy, or like images projected at a sharp angle onto a surface, this angle however much less sharp than in the case of the
boy's arm mentioned above, traces of the space they have left
behind sticking like dirt to the shoes of the three figures, especially their heels, collected in clumps, making it hard for them to
tread, traces of the objects they have left behind carried along
by their bodies as if by mighty currents of matter, for instance
sliding mud or molten lava—bricks that were part of buildings they have walked by, windows, doors, fences, gates in them,
posts on which clotheslines are strung, clotheslines themselves,
laundry hung out to dry on the clotheslines, telephone posts,
street lamp posts, posts on which street signs are displayed, letters from such signs, traffic lights, sidewalk curbs, trees growing
along streets, people passed in streets, their glances, curious or
bored, their clothes, usually shabby, sometimes decent, outlines
of their bodies, fat or skinny, in rare cases attractive, bicycles,
motorbikes, passenger cars, pickup trucks, trailer trucks, and

so forth. The front parts of the bodies of the three travelers (Nelson Fitipaldo does not see them but he knows what they look like) bear the mark of what lies ahead of them, that is, the vast empty space, endless, cold, its temperature very close to absolute zero, 0 °K, -273.15 °C, -459.67 °F, in other words, already frozen solid in places, especially the eyes, the mother's in particular—all white and blue, covered with concentric circles, immobile, expressionless, like eyes of dead fish.

9. epilogue

Nelson Fitipaldo stands at the window of his kitchen-apartment and looks outside. An unhealthy reddish color tinges the world like blood dissolved in water. There are three cars parked in the narrow paved passageway leading to the car garages on the right, all of them squeezed against the rusty chain-link fence running along the property line—two of them facing left and one right. A small dog is stuck facing away from the building, apparently forever, in a hole in the fence, rusty like the fence itself. Beyond the athletic field on the other side of the fence, in the distance, between the houses that look like garbage strewn haphazardly over the flat land, among the laundry hung out to dry on clotheslines, hangs limply a small rectangle of the worn, faded blue, percale sky. The soccer field is empty, its right side dissolving in the void like a painting in water. There is no sign of the goal left on that side. The players are all gone and in their place remain holes so that the field looks like a piece of old cloth badly eaten by moths. The long jumper has finally landed in the sand pit at the edge of the precipice on the right and is desperately trying to balance himself so as not to fall forward into the emptiness before him.

THE jOYS AnD SORROWS
OF R. YORK

l. r. york's fiancée comes to see him

The bus undulated through the evening air like a golden carp working its way through water, its body bending this way and that, wrinkles forming on its shiny metal skin first on one side, then on the other, the air making a swishing sound as it slid past, vacuum gurgling behind it, trees next to the road swaying like seaweed after it had passed.

From time to time the strong hand of the breeze would brutally peel back the neck of her loose dress and move down between her breasts and the bare midriff all the way to where her thighs met to rest for a moment on the soft triangle of her pubic hair. It seemed to have a need to reassure itself of the latter's existence and of its rights of ownership to it. She remembered the cold, rectangular stare of the mirror in her room as she paused naked for an instant before it while getting ready to go out.

Children led balloons on long strings like placid, well-behaved sky dogs while their parents, usually fathers, led them by their hands along the neatly paved park paths. The red, blue, yellow, white, etc., pear-shaped forms played hide and seek among the huge, sloppy, Rorschach inkblot shapes of the green leaves. On white benches, turned into comfortable orthopedic shapes by rows of parallel wooden slats, situated at regular intervals on both sides of the paths old people, aged eighty, ninety, or even one hundred, sat, awaiting the arrival of their peaceful ends. Amorous couples had all merged into incongruous, improbable forms, locked in tight embraces and passionate kisses that would never end. In the distance between the tree trunks the clear space could be seen tilting clumsily now this way, now that, like grossly obese persons with no talent for dancing, to the sound of brass bands.

In a cemetery on a hill the bus passed, an ethnic festival was taking place, probably a Slavic one, and sounds of spirited music and singing could be heard streaming from that direction. Occasionally an arm or a leg dressed in red or white would shoot up among the tops of the trees moving skyward, accompanied by an exclamation that sounded like "hey" or "oy." It would descend quickly to where it came from however, unable to hold on to its hard-won height.

Around the round plazas buses would be seen driving around in circles, their tires screeching wildly, bodies dangerously leaning out, about to topple over, their drivers having gone mad with happiness, sitting behind the steering wheels with their heads thrown back and mouths open wide like windows in houses in northern countries on the first warm day after a long winter. A detachment of cavalry was riding through one of the squares, about twenty men on horses as tall as trees, dressed in red and blue uniforms, shiny black boots, black patent leather belts, golden and black helmets, sabers in their hands, their blades fiercely guarding the riders' cheeks. The droppings the horses left behind were like perfectly shaped, shiny bronze balls scattered on the pavement. The images of the horses' hoofs appeared and disappeared in the immaculately clean, polished cobblestones like the sounds of footsteps echoing in empty corridors.

In sidewalk cafés beer sighed mysteriously like dense forests as it spilled over the edges of the heavy mugs.

He waited for her by the carousel, having just jumped off it like its tangent, and whispered "You blew my mind" as he bent forward to kiss her. A night bird flew out of her hair touching his forehead with its soft dark wing before disappearing in the trees. He was to remember it for the rest of his life.

They both remembered also for the rest of their lives the tall thin man with an ashen complexion, blue circles under his eyes, sunken cheeks, and a huge chest puffed out like a male pigeon's crop, who dove off the hundred-foot-tall tower to land in a basin of water no more than six inches deep and lived to receive the applause of the handful of people who had gathered in a semicircle around him. He stood in his skimpy swimming trunks, his feet together in the cramped container in the shallow water, bending mutely in the three directions to thank his admirers.

At night the electric lights bled painlessly like wounds in water amidst the thick black foliage and until the break of dawn the sea beyond the trees bloomed on the cubist rocks with the giant cubist peonies of its waves.

2. a dress rehearsal

R. York and his wife Olive (for "Olive Oyl," because she resembles the character both physically and otherwise in an uncanny way) on the stage of a public school before a dress rehearsal of a play in which their four-year-old daughter Laura is to take part. The stage empty except for the couple and the child, other parents and children momentarily hidden behind the curtains on both sides. The set represents Dutch countryside with a peasant cottage—white walls, red roof, door, and window—on the left, and a windmill—also white walls, red roof, door, windows, and wings—on the right. Red and white tulips sticking up artificially prim and proper in two rectangular flower beds on both sides of the stage. A blue, cloudless sky in the background. All three characters front center stage, the adults facing each other—R. York left, his wife right—a couple of feet apart, the child between them, facing the auditorium, examining with interest a red apple she is holding in her hands. The parents dressed in ordinary street clothes, the girl in a white dress, trimmed with blue, a blue apron, and white shoes. Blue ribbons at the end of each of her two rat-tail braids.

R. York (*pleading*): But she looks lovely in her....

R. York's wife (*angry*): It's not a question of how she looks, it's what she's supposed to wear! I sewed the costume for her and you were supposed to dress her in it and bring her here. What are we going to do now?

R. York: But she doesn't look nice in red and white....

R. York's wife: She does so, and it doesn't matter anyway! She's supposed to wear the same costume all the other girls are wearing.

R. York: Dutch is associated with blue and white.... Look at all the pictures...Dutch chocolate, the chocolate liquor bottle, china.... That's why I suggested a Dutch theme.

R. York's wife: Theme-shmeme.... Who cares? The artist thought red and white was better!

R. York: But red and white is Danish, not Dutch.... Look at their soccer team's uniforms in the World Cup final...I mean playoffs.... And Polish, I think, although Poland didn't make it to the playoffs...not in the last one, anyway....

R. York's wife: What's that got to do with it?... Go! Get in the car and bring the costume!

R. York: It'll be too late.

R. York's wife: No, it won't. People aren't ready yet. It'll take another half an hour.

R. York: I won't be able to make it.

R. York's wife: Yes, you will. It takes only about ten minutes to get home from here, even in traffic, and it's late now. There's no traffic. You'll get there in five minutes and will be back in ten. We'll have plenty of time to change her.

R. York: I'm not going. You go!

R. York's wife: Why?

R. York: Because she looks OK this way...better in fact.... And blue goes well with red and white.... Tricolor...French.

R. York's wife: But this isn't a play about France, it's about Holland.... I mean it takes place in Holland.... You dreamt it up yourself.

R. York: I'm changing my mind now....

R. York's wife (*turning red with anger*): You can't change your mind at a dress rehearsal.... (*Doesn't know what to say, beside herself with exasperation.*)

R. York: I've just done it, so there.... But if you want to, you can go. I'm not stopping you. I'll stay with her.

R. York's wife: I can't! I'm supposed to help out with the play!

R. York: I'll help out instead.

R. York's wife: You won't know what to do.

R. York: Big deal! I'll learn.

R. York's wife (*apoplectic*): Christ almighty! Just go! Get the dress and bring it here!

R. York (*rock of Gibraltar*): You go. I'll stay.

R. York's wife (*half coherent*): You're crazy…crazy as a loon…. All that blue and white stuff…. It's making me sick…. It's everywhere…. I can't stand it anymore…. I'll puke next time I see a blue and white flower, or a piece of china, or a car….

R. York (*his wife has hit a raw spot*): So you don't like our new car? That's why you don't want to go?… You don't want to drive it?

R. York's wife screams a primal scream of exasperation.

There are signs of people about to come out onto the stage from behind the curtains on both sides of it to see what is going on. The girl Laura is totally absorbed in inspecting the apple. It looks like she might grow up to be a botanist.

3. man jumping into water
After a painting by Jurij Solovij

R. York in his psychiatrist's office during one of his sessions. He sits in a contemporary-styled armchair made from teakwood, with spindly arms and legs and foam rubber cushions upholstered in a plaid material, green, yellow, and red. The psychiatrist, Dr. MacGregor, sits in the opposite corner on the left in a huge, overstuffed, red imitation leather reclining chair with a footrest. The chair stands a little away from the wall so that he can lean back in it, which is what he is doing. He has a red walrus mustache, very thick and bristly, and wears shotglass-bottom eyeglasses. In his left hand he is holding a spiral-bound notebook and in his right a ballpoint pen. Both of them lie in his lap. His head is hung down, with his chin resting on his chest, so that he looks asleep. A couch that matches the chair R. York is sitting in, without armrests but with a cushion on the end close to him, stands on his right. On his left, opposite R. York, is a window, with drawn white venetian blinds on it. The shadow of a branch of the tree growing outside the window falls on the blinds, forming a pattern reminiscent of a Japanese print. R. York is holding onto the arms of the chair with his hands, clutching them tightly so that they have grown white, as if he were in a dentist's office and the dentist were working on him, or as if the chair were inclined over a precipice and he was afraid of slipping off it. The sharp edges of the armrests hurt his hands and he has a feeling they are human bones. The bones seem to be his own, inside his body, so that he seems to be holding onto his own bones. He is narrating a dream he had since his last session.

R. York (*continuing*): ...and it's like there're these cliffs all around the lake, or maybe not cliffs but high bluffs of bare clay eroded by water, so that they've sharp edges on top, and up and down, where water has run down.... They're brown, but not like clay, except shiny, as if they've been painted with glossy paint like walls in a room. And I have a feeling I'm in

a room, like a dining room, cramped, like in a lower middle-
class person's home, after a Sunday dinner…. But the lake is
big, and I can see only the cliffs, I mean bluffs, on the other
side of it, but still I feel all hemmed in, enclosed, like in my, I
mean some middle-class person's cramped dining room. And
it seems a middle-class person's dining room because I have
a feeling I've just had a typical middle-class Sunday dinner of
meat and mashed potatoes, lots of them, and can still hear the
strains of a Brahms composition, a string quartet or something
like that, being played on the radio, because I associate Brahms
with middle-class tastes….

The surface of the lake shines like thick paint, not like water,
and it's also brown, so that it seems that it was with this paint
that the walls, I mean the cliffs, I mean the bluffs, were painted.
There're no ripples on the surface, the way it would be with
paint, so it's definitely not water…it's too thick to ripple. I'm
standing on the level of the water, I mean the paint…the lake,
so the cliffs, I mean bluffs, must be behind me. So that's probably why I have a feeling of being closed in. They're probably
towering above me…just behind me. I'm like probably ten feet
away from the edge of the water, I mean the shore, of the lake.
In front of me, a little to the right, right on the edge of the
shore, stands a man, facing the lake, taller than me, and thin.
He's wearing an undershirt and pants, and suddenly he starts
taking them off. He takes his undershirt off first and throws it
down on the ground next to him. There're more clothes there,
so he must have been wearing more clothes and he's taken
them off already. And when he takes his shirt off I can see his
back. It's very broad, but extremely thin, sort of hollow, caved
in, with huge shoulder blades, like wings…butterfly wings, and

he seems to be able to fly on them as if he were a butterfly. His skin is brown too, like the paint, but he's not black, not an African, I mean, only tanned this way, but not from the sun, except from time and exposure, like a mummy, a body buried in ice or a marsh for a long time.... He's bald on top, and the bald spot is light, sort of yellow and white, so that's why he's not a black...and his hair is straight too.... So then he takes his pants off. He wears no belt, so he just unbuttons them up front and unzips them, and takes them off, and throws them down on the ground.... I'm not sure if he's naked underneath or is wearing something...jockey shorts or a loincloth.... If he is, then the thing is sort of yellow and white...like the bald spot.... But maybe it's his skin.... Maybe he is naked after all.... And then he bends down in sort of a queer way, just at the waist, as if trying to touch his toes, like exercising, but in reality he's preparing to dive into the lake, into the paint, the water.... And then I notice how really thin he is...like a skeleton, literally skin and bones.... You can see this especially in his legs, in the back. The skin is stretched tight, and under it you can see the bones protruding. There's nothing around them, he's all empty inside, just bones, with the skin around them. And the bones stick out on the hips...the pelvic bones.... The skin is torn on one side there, on the left hip, and you can see the bone sticking out there...white and yellow, like the bald spot on his head....

Way in the distance the sun is setting over the cliffs...or maybe the water, the lake itself.... So maybe the lake isn't all surrounded by bluffs...not way in the distance.... And it's just a very bright yellow and red spot there, and it's reflected in the paint, the surface of the lake, and it also illuminates the other, the right hip of the man....

And there're more people around me, somewhere on my right, although I can't see them.... They're like a team, a television crew who've come to film what the man is doing....

The psychiatrist (*after R. York has not said anything for a while*): Why?... Why are they filming it?

R. York (*after some hesitation*): Because it's interesting...noteworthy....

The psychiatrist: Noteworthy in what way?

R. York (*after hesitating longer*): I don't know.... Unusual.... He's strange looking, and the lake is strange....

The psychiatrist: So they're filming him because he's strange?

R. York (*with more certainty*): No...because he's jumping into the water...the lake....

The psychiatrist (*smiling*): OK. Because he's jumping into the water.... What is he going to do there? Swim?

R. York: No!

The psychiatrist: Then what? Bathe?

R. York (*more hesitant*): Nnooo...I don't know....

The psychiatrist: (*grinning*): Is he going to be long under the water...the paint?

R. York (*hesitates for a long time*): I don't know....

The psychiatrist (*becoming serious*): No matter. (*Sitting up and directing his bristling mustache toward R. York, as if to prod him.*) And what have you brought along today? Let's see.... I can see you've got something in your pocket. (*He leans toward R. York as if planning to retrieve physically what R. York has.*)

R. York (*blushing*): I.... A photograph and flowers....

The psychiatrist: A photograph and flowers.... Let's see them.

R. York sticks his hand into his pants pocket and pulls out a crumpled photograph and something wrapped in a handkerchief. He sits up and extends them over to the psychiatrist as if thinking the man could reach across the room.

The psychiatrist (*laughing*): No, no, I don't want to look at them. You tell me about them. Tell me what's in the photograph.

R. York (*looking at the photograph*): It's a shot of me when I was about nine months old...sitting on the sofa....

The psychiatrist: What do you look like?

R. York: I'm chubby and bleary-eyed...bald...surprisingly like the way I look now.... Naked.... Clutching a rattle....

The psychiatrist (*intrigued*): A rattle?... What sort of a rattle?

R. York: White and gray...I mean blue.... It's gray in the photograph, because it's in black and white, but I think it was blue....

The psychiatrist: White and blue...hmmm.... (*Makes a note in his notebook.*) And what are the flowers like?

R. York unwraps the handkerchief in which there lie a few wilted white and blue violets and pansies and looks at them with pity. They seem tears with which the handkerchief has been stained.

R. York: White and blue...from my garden.... (*Looks up suddenly.*) But they're too small....

4. porto penal

Porto Penal was where R. York lost his daughter. She was five at the time and she drowned in the sea while the family was there on vacation.

The following takes place the morning of the drowning shortly before R. York finds out about it.

R. York stands outside the door of his motel room ready to go to the beach. The motel is a long single-storied structure with a flat roof built out of cinder blocks, painted gray, and resembles a concentration camp barrack. Porto Penal is on Portugal's Atlantic coast, situated on a C-shaped bay surrounded by tall basalt cliffs. Stone was mined from these once by prisoners from the local penal colony, hence the name— "Penal Port." The colony is long gone but it has left its imprint on the town's architecture—all of its buildings are low and plain in a numbingly depressive way without any of the grace associated with architecture of Mediterranean countries and those that neighbor them. This applies even to the town church which looks more like a giant tomb than a church, with its stubby rectangular stone cross on top. The motel is located on the north end of the bay which is slightly elevated over the rest of it and from there the town looks like a vast cemetery with giant rectangular tombs.

R. York and his wife and daughter are staying in adjoining rooms. R. York's wife likes to sleep late and he gets up early so she sleeps with their daughter and he by himself. It is nine thirty in the morning. R. York has slept unusually late because of being inexplicably tired the night before. On waking up he put his ear to the wall to check if anyone on the other side was stirring but heard no sound and assumed his wife and daughter were still asleep. Sometimes they stay in bed until noon.

R. York is wearing his knee-length white nightshirt over his black swimming trunks and a pair of black loafers on his bare feet and is carrying a rolled-up white towel under his left arm together with a long black umbrella. He goes like this to the beach all the time because he forgot to bring from home a beach robe, sandals, and a bath towel and so uses his nightshirt, regular shoes, and a motel towel instead. He brought from home the umbrella because he had been warned it rains in Portugal in the summer and takes it along to the beach to make himself look more like an Indian. The first time he went to the beach without it he felt he looked silly. He saw men in Indian movies dressed in long white shirts and regular shoes carrying umbrellas and thought he would pretend to be Indian. He is thinking in particular of the movie *Two Daughters* by the Bengali filmmaker Satyajit Ray. In addition the umbrella comes in handy—it protects him from sun and wind when they are strong. In his right hand R. York carries a tube of toothpaste. He is inordinately fond of mints, has exhausted his supply of them, and has been unable to get any in town. On waking up he felt strangely anxious and because mints make him feel better he had to put some toothpaste in his mouth. The taste of mint lingering from having just brushed his teeth gave him this idea and the solution proved to be mildly effective. He has a feeling he will be needing more taste of mint on the beach and therefore is bringing the toothpaste along.

The small black Seat (a Spanish version of Fiat) he has rented and a beat-up gray French Simca belonging to the clients in the adjacent room are parked in front of the motel door and he has squeezed his way between them and has stopped before deciding what to do. Contrary to what he has expected it is cold and overcast with the clouds high and arranged in narrow parallel rows like bodies laid out on a cement floor in a warehouse or a hangar after a devastating natural disaster. Hopeful, R. York turns around searching for the sun and squints in preparation of seeing it. The sky is overcast as much behind him as up front however and he realizes he will not be sunning himself today on the beach. For an instant he thinks he might go back to his room and wait for his wife and daughter to wake up but decides against it. He finds the room depressing and although it is overcast and cold the beach will definitely be more pleasant. His umbrella will help. The cliffs are about a hundred feet away from the motel and to his surprise he notices that a big roll of barbed wire runs along their edge on top; they rise about a hundred feet above ground at this point. The barbed wire runs as far along the edge of the cliffs as he can see and he assumes it continues all the way around the bay. He doesn't remember noticing it since coming to Porto Penal and concludes it must have been laid down during the night or that morning. It seems very strange for something like this to have happened and he doesn't know what to think. No matter which is true—either the barbed wire being there before and his not noticing it or it having been laid down since the day before—it is extremely unlikely.

Upset by the barbed wire R. York gets a burning urge to read in the Bible. He is not a devout Christian, has never had such an urge before, and has not even read the Bible since his days in school, but he feels he has to do it now and is determined to satisfy his wish. He feels there must be a Bible in his room because he recalls reading or hearing somewhere that the Gideons leave Bibles in hotels all over the world, not only in English-speaking countries. He quickly goes back to his room, looks in the drawer in the bedside table, but there is no Bible there. He looks everywhere else in the room including under the blankets in the closet and under the mattress but still finds no Bible. This annoys and amazes him and he almost decides he will have to give up on the idea of reading in the Bible but then thinks of the motel office. He feels they must have a Bible there—Portugal is a Catholic country after all. He rushes out of the room and heads for the motel office, which is located at the end of the building on his right. He has been there before when they have checked in. It is a room like all the others ex-cept it is being used for an office.

The owner/manager of the motel is Dom Rodrigo. R. York finds him in the office bent over a stack of papers on top of his desk. Dom Rodrigo stands up when R. York comes in and waits for him to come closer and to his surprise R. York thinks Dom Rodrigo looks Indian. He has never thought this before and is surprised he didn't but now he is certain Dom Rodrigo is Indian. He explains to himself Dom Rodrigo must be from the former Portuguese colony of Goa and moved to Portugal when it was incorporated into India. Dom Rodrigo does have some features common to Indian men—swarthy skin, dark eyes, and straight black hair—and right now he is wearing a white shirt with an open collar and a pair of dark pants as men in India might do but all of this has nothing to do with R. York's feeling. It is motivated by his pretending to be Indian; he had never been to see Dom Rodrigo in the outfit he is wearing before. He would like to explore this subject further but decides to turn to what made him come to the office. It is more important.

R. York doesn't speak Portuguese and Dom Rodrigo doesn't speak English so R. York resorts to speaking in short phrases as he has done on previous occasions when he has had to communicate with Dom Rodrigo.

"A Bible?" asks R. York looking Dom Rodrigo in the eyes and trying to shape his hands into a gesture implying a question as best he can under the circumstances. (He is still holding the towel and umbrella under his left arm and the tube of toothpaste in his right hand.)

Dom Rodrigo has no idea what that means. He stares back mutely at R. York with a blank expression on his face.

R. York repeats the phrase and when it is received by Dom Rodrigo in the same way he remembers that "Biblia" is a Latin word and as far as he knows is used in all Romance languages. He also has a rudimentary understanding of the use of articles in Spanish.

"Una Biblia?" asks R. York still looking Dom Rodrigo in the eyes.

"Uma Biblia?" replies Dom Rodrigo his face lighting up at realizing finally what R. York is after and converting R. York's Spanish into Portuguese. "No," he continues. "No Biblia." He doesn't have a copy of the Bible in his office.

R. York is surprised at this and for an instant resigns himself to the idea of not being able to realize his dream of reading in the Bible this morning. His being revolts against this however and his mind frantically searches for a solution. The Indian theme is still alive in his mind and he remembers the two great Sanskrit classics "Ramayana" and "Mahabharata." He imagines them as great big books like the Bible, forgets that it was for the purpose of reading that he wanted the Bible and not for its size, thinks of the latter as only a big book, remembers that he feels Dom Rodrigo might be from India, thinks he might have one or both of the works, and staring Dom Rodrigo in the eyes blurts out "Ramayana?" and them "Mahabharata?" He has heard these names pronounced by Indians and knows a little about Indian languages, so in the first word he puts the accent on the second syllable ("RamAyana") and enunciates the "r's" in both in the retroflex way with the tip of his tongue rolled back and pressed against the roof of his mouth.

Dom Rodrigo is baffled by what R. York has said. His face now is not blank but creased with an expression of deep puzzlement. He clearly is not from India. R. York has decided he has lost and must give up. Dejected he lets his eyes drift aside and they focus on the bookcase that stands to the left of the desk against the wall. Among the books he sees there is a big thick one in hard red cover with gold lettering on its back. To him it looks like a Bible and he forgets what Dom Rodrigo has just said and is full of hope again his wish might be satisfied after all. He moves toward the bookcase with his hand extended for the book and giving Dom Rodrigo a quick looks says, "Una Biblia? Si?" (He did not notice Dom Rodrigo had said "uma" instead of "una.")

Dom Rodrigo says nothing, not sure of what R. York has in mind, but when the latter picks up the book, realizing what is going on, says, smiling and wagging his finger: "No Biblia...no.... *Lusíadas*." It is a deluxe edition of the Portuguese national epic *Os Lusíadas* by Camões.

R. York realizes he has made a mistake when he opens the book. It is not a Bible. The text in it is arranged in stanzas however and since passages in the Bible are commonly referred to as "verses" he feels the book might serve him well after all. He couldn't have understood much of the Bible in Portuguese anyway so he will probably not get much less from this book. He will try reading in it and will see what happens.

With gestures and broken English he asks Dom Rodrigo if he can take the book to the beach. The latter readily agrees and R. York, finally happy, walks out of the office pressing the book together with the tube of toothpaste to his chest.

The ground in front of the motel is covered with sand and gravel. They crunch dryly under R. York's feet making his skin crawl as if from someone scratching a blackboard with his fingernails. The land slopes gently toward the sea, which lies some three hundred feet away. A paved two-lane road separates the motel grounds from the beach. It is some thirty feet away from the motel and curves gently to the right as it approaches the town following the arc of the bay. The road emerges suddenly from behind the cliffs that come up all the way to it at this end and disappears just as suddenly behind them at the other as if relieved it has managed to sneak through the town unharmed.

R. York thinks about the book he is carrying, imagining how he is going to read it. He expects to feel gloomy doing it because of the many "oo" sounds in Portuguese. He has been feeling gloomy since coming to Portugal and attributes it to this feature of the language.

R. York stops when he comes to the road. A car has just emerged from behind the cliffs on his right and is speeding toward town. It is about two hundred feet away and he doesn't feel he would be able to cross the road safely. The car is black and strangely shaped, with rounded edges and windows only up front. It looks a little like a hearse but R. York observes it could just as well be an ambulance because in a country whose language sounds so gloomy it wouldn't be strange for ambulances to be black.

While waiting for the car to pass, R. York looks at the bay. The beach is flat all along and uniformly wide, the same as in front of the motel. It is empty of people except about a third of the way down, almost in the center of town, a small crowd, per-haps twenty people, has gathered in one spot on the edge of the water marring its emptiness like a cluster of flyspecks on an otherwise spotlessly clean mirror. They seem to be looking down at something—it isn't certain if it is already on the sand or still being pulled out of the water. R. York imagines it to be a monstrous sea creature like the one in the final scene in Fellini's *La Dolce Vita*. He wishes he could see it but decides he will not go to the trouble of walking all the way there. He will hide under the umbrella and try to read the book.

Way in the distance where the bay ends and the road disappears behind the cliffs can be seen the weird rock formation called Pai Preto—"Black Father"—resembling a man with a wide-rimmed hat on his head staring into distance—a male equiva-lent of a female figure waiting in vain for the return from the sea of her fisherman husband or son.

5. flying dogs

Through his sleep R. York could hear the flying dogs barking and so he opened his eyes and saw one of them alight at that very moment on top of a tree right in front of him. The dog was all black, without any features, as if a silhouette cut out of a sheet of black paper, probably because it was seen on the background of the light sky. It had a muscular but not a very big body, all smooth, apparently short-haired, powerful paws, a long and thin, flexible tail, short snout with big jowls, and huge ears, almost like those of an elephant, with the aid of which he flew by flapping them like wings. While still landing, it stretched out its head and snapped its jaws at something—R.

York assumed an insect of some kind. It looked like the insect got away for the dog didn't go on chewing. The branch under it bent as its paws caught it and the dog sagged way down as though it were going to fall off but in the end held onto the branch, its paws apparently equipped with powerful talons as befits a big bird—after all, it was a *flying* dog and so a dog-*bird* as much as a bird-*dog*. The top of the tree swayed up and down a few times but then steadied and the dog stayed on it looking around, apparently for another insect to catch. It barked a few times as if out of frustration and the bark sounded like the cawing of an irascible crow.

Having had enough of the dog, R. York lowered his eyes and saw he was lying on top of a long, narrow wooden table in the backyard of a peasant house which was on his right—long and low, with white walls and a high blue roof, and three square windows, completely black, making it look like a weird, deformed skull with three eye sockets. There were trees all around it, tall and dense, and from the darkness under them or perhaps from around the corner of the house a tall, slender figure emerged and headed toward him. It was a girl in a long light dress, with long weeping-willow hair, and when she came up to R. York and stopped, looking at him in a friendly way with her huge daisy eyes, a wistful smile on her lips, he realized it was his daughter Laura come back from the dead.

"Laurie," he said, raising himself on his elbow, his voice trembling and his eyes filling with tears, "you've come back…. I'm so glad to see you…."

He sat up and she came closer to him and put her arm around him without saying a word—so gently, it felt like a breeze; and it felt cool from then on as if it were a breeze constantly blowing.

"Hug me tighter," R. York said, exasperated, putting his arms around her, but they went through her as if through air—through a gust of wind. All of a sudden she was no longer by him but a few feet away from the table. She looked at him with the same sad-happy smile on her lips but her eyes were expressionless as a pair of daisies.

"You've grown so much," R. York said, trying to forget what had just happened, glad to find something happy to talk about.

She nodded her head, the Mona-Lisa smile persisting on her lips, and R. York extended his hand toward her as if not remembering what had just happened. She wafted her hand past his once more like a gentle breeze and made a motion as if to leave.

"You have to go?" R. York asked sadly, knowing what the answer would be.

She nodded her head and the smile on her lips changed a little, turning sadder than before.

Then she turned right and while keeping her eyes on him started to walk, turning her head more and more to the left while moving, so as to see him. And he also sat up higher and kept turning at first his head and then his torso to the left so as not to lose sight of her. Finally it was too uncomfortable for her, and so she raised her hand and waved, and then turned her head forward, gradually disappearing in the darkness under the trees.

Mechanically, he also waved, although her back was now turned to him, and when he could no longer see her he turned right, hung his feet down, and sat like that, not knowing what to do. It was then that he heard the flying dogs barking again, like crows cawing, having a fight, and concluded they must have been at it all along but he had only now noticed.

6. r. york goes to see his wife

One day R. York went to see his wife. She lived on the other side of town and R. York had to change buses twice to get there. It was in late spring and the weather was beautiful. Streets were flooded with warm air and looked like rooms with their windows wide open for the first time after a long, hard winter. City squares (all round) were packed with people unwilling to move on to where their duties and obligations awaited them. Many of those at bus stops would not notice their bus had arrived and would be left standing vacant-eyed and with mouths open, as if in a trance, after it drove off. At gas stations many of the attendants, in their gray-striped uniforms that looked like those of convicts, still had their sizable hero sandwiches stuck in their breast pockets, having forgotten to consume them during their lunch hour which had passed a long time ago.

On the first bus the driver acted very strangely. Time and again, sometimes within a matter of seconds, he would swat himself with his hand on the nose or, less frequently, other parts of the face, as if trying to kill a fly that had settled there. A few times during the ride he pulled the bus over to the side, put on the hand brake, got a flyswatter from under his seat, and mumbling something angrily went down the aisle swatting in different directions after invisible and almost certainly nonexistent flies. Usually he would swat the air but a few times he hit the walls of the bus, backs of seats, and even passengers, apparently thinking he saw a fly there. Those passengers that were hit didn't protest however, obviously understanding the situation, and pretended nothing had happened. The bus driver was cross-eyed, so that it was hard to guess where he was looking, and each time he passed by, R. York was afraid he would be hit with the swatter and then wouldn't know what to do, but fortunately it did not happen.

On the second bus many of the passengers looked like apes— gorillas, to be precise. Their skin wasn't black, but gray, the color of milk and ashes, yet smooth and shiny, as if polished with wax. Their hair was coal black, straight, short, and very thick, so that you couldn't see the skin under it. It seemed to grow over most of their bodies, including in the case of women and children. Their skulls were pointed, foreheads receding, faces flat, noses practically non-existent, chins also receding, teeth forming a sharp projecting angle, lips also practically nonexistent, necks short, backs hunched, shoulders sloping, torsos massive, arms long, legs short and bent at the knees. They walked in a shuffle and had deep guttural voices, which actually sounded pleasant. Their eyes also projected a keen intelligence like those of some animals and R. York was afraid to look into them, thinking the people would guess he thought they looked like apes. He was afraid they would beat him up for that. He was sure he wasn't a match for them, including many of the women and children, and he hated to think what would be left of him if he had gotten into a fight with one—any—of the men. He wondered who the people were and where they had come from because he had never seen or heard of them before. He would have liked to call them strangers—recent immigrants from some exotic distant country or an obscure indigenous strain which had recently become incorporated into the society—but this was clearly not so since their language was totally unaccented and grammatically correct—more correct in fact than that of most native speakers he knew, including himself, as R. York observed—and he found it a pleasure to listen to it. In the end he gave up trying to guess who the people were, deciding it didn't matter. They were there and that was all. They seemed to have settled in the part of town the second bus ran through for most of the passengers on that bus were of this type and there were many similar-looking people in the streets.

There was nothing unusual about the third bus except that its driver acted normal and there were none of the ape-like people on it.

R. York's wife rented a furnished room in a big old wooden house. It had a tall ceiling and bare walls painted a shiny dark green. The floor in the room was painted a reddish brown but was badly scuffed up. All of the wooden trim, including the door to the hallway, that of the closet, and the window frame, was varnished dark brown and looked in good condition however. There was a narrow metal bed painted to imitate wood against one of the longer walls, a longish wooden table with a plain, worn top, and a likewise plain and old wooden chair next to it. A rectangular mirror, badly faded, as if seen by a person with bad eyesight, once more with a plain and worn wooden frame, hung above the table.

There were neither curtains nor a shade on the window and an incredibly strong and obstinate sunlight was forcing its way into the room. When R. York and his wife made love a while later after he arrived, the sunlight, which shone on the bed, made it uncomfortable for the two as if it were a huge rectangular piece of plywood, stood upright, they had to contend with while trying to enjoy themselves. It seemed to have very sharp edges.

As was her custom R. York's wife kept her legs up in the air during the intercourse and the heel of her right foot rubbed against the wall above the bed as she was rocked back and forth by her husband. A shiny, seemingly greasy spot, was left there from the many intercourses the two had engaged in.

It was excruciatingly hot in the room and the act was like a long bout with a fever for R. York and, it seemed, his wife. Her face was bright red under him, swollen with blood to the point of being practically featureless, like a giant, elongated, and extremely ripe tomato.

Afterwards R. York stood by the window in his undershirt and boxer shorts, smoking, blowing the smoke out the window, looking into the backyard. It was sizable but ninety percent of it was taken up by a chestnut tree, dark and vast as the night, that gave off a stink like a mouth with halitosis. A swing was suspended from one of its branches and an idiot boy, seventeen or eighteen, very pale and fat, sat on it swinging absentmindedly back and forth, with his feet on the ground. His lips were pink and wet, and stuck in a couple of places even though his mouth was open, making him look like the woman in the red hat in the well-known picture by Vermeer.

7. r. york gets electrocuted (giant flowers)

R. York's job was to take care of the grounds. This consisted of fertilizing, watering, and mowing the grass between the transformers and towers, and under the power lines, and edging it along concrete walks, as well as sweeping the walks and keeping them clean from ice and snow in the winter. No raking of leaves was necessary since there were no trees growing inside the grounds and the walls were too tall to permit any leaves to come in from the outside. The climate during those years had gotten very mild and there wasn't much snow in the wintertime. As a consequence R. York had little to do during the fall and winter. When he had nothing to do and the weather was nice during that time he would sun himself, standing, squatting, or sitting on the concrete walks. When it rained or snowed he would stand or squat in a corner formed by the walls. For this he preferred a particular one. It was less than ninety degrees and he was able to squeeze himself more snugly into it and thus keep warm and dry. The reason the corner was less than ninety degrees was due to a miscalculation on the part of the surveyors. The fertilizing, watering, and edging were relatively small parts of R. York's duties. As a consequence the bulk of them consisted of mowing the grass and taking care of the lawn mower. The latter required a lot of maintenance and preventive work. R. York had to check it regularly and order parts for it that looked worn in advance so that he wouldn't have to wait for them when the lawn mower broke. He would then have a difficult time catching up with the mowing. The few times that it had broken unexpectedly he was lucky enough to be able to fix it within a matter of hours. As a consequence he was able to catch up with the mowing. The grounds were enormous and the mower small, and it took R. York about three days to mow all the grass. When he was done with it, it would be time for him to start over again unless he had to fertilize, water, edge, or take care of the lawn mower. Those distractions from the mowing were a burden on R. York and sometimes he had to work late into the evening to keep up with the chore of cutting the grass. He thus kept himself busy for a good part of the year—about eight months out of twelve.

R. York loved his job. The power station was an oasis of peace and order in a frantic and unpredictable world and he would look at the gray, twenty-foot-tall brick walls surrounding the grounds as a child looks at adult family members who make sure nothing bad ever happens to it. Faint noises of the traffic, construction sites, and occasional hysterical voices of people would reach his ears, but they would actually make him feel cozy rather than threatened. They reminded him that he was protected on all sides by the walls, which would never let the hostile forces from the outside come near him.

R. York's supervisor stayed inside a huge hall in the power station building that constituted one of the four walls surrounding the grounds. It was reached in three steps, at the top of which was a wide but narrow platform, at the end of which in turn was a glass wall with a door in it. The hall was three stories tall—as tall as the building—and its floor was of polished marble that shone like water. R. York was reluctant to tread on it, afraid he would sink, and the sensation never left him even though every time he put his foot down he found a hard surface under it. He never got any feeling of elation from walking on it however, never felt like Christ walking on water.

The supervisor was called Warden Warren. He sat at a huge, old-fashioned, gray metal desk, facing the glass wall so that he could see R. York work. He apparently wasn't bored by his job because there was never any book, newspaper, or document on the desk. He also didn't spend much time on the phone because there wasn't one on the desk; there was one on the wall on his left however, and he would get up, walk to it, and pick it up when it rang, and he used it for making calls when he had to speak to someone. Otherwise he just sat there with his hands in his lap or on the desk, staring ahead. He probably wasn't always keeping his eyes on R. York.

One evening in late May R. York was still mowing the grass. He had taken some time off that day to service the mower and had to finish his day's quota of cutting grass. He still had about an hour of work left. It was pleasantly warm and humid and the air felt like a soothing ointment on R. York's skin. His nostrils were filled with the acrid smell of cut grass he loved so much. He could have gone on working like that for hours. The three walls and the power station building were there, faithfully guarding his peace on all sides, and the narrow concrete paths were white against the deep green grass, running off obediently in all directions, carrying a message to the four corners of the grounds that R. York was coming with the lawn mower as fast as he could. The transformers in their rectangular boxes hummed faithfully their monotonous melody, the tall towers rose gracefully into the air like so many rubber balls bouncing off a hard surface all at once, and the power lines sagged gently between them like the bellies of horses dozing after a good feeding. High above, the sky was a giant, slightly worn and faded, blue percale sheet sagging in unison with the power lines.

There must have been a short in one of the transformers and the humid air must have acted as a better conductor, for at one point, as R. York accidentally touched with the lawnmower the corner of the transformer box he was mowing around, he was struck with a bolt of electricity from above. An instant prior to this a wisp of hair in the very center on top of his head stood up as if in fear of what was coming and then an enormous discharge, like a giant, jagged corkscrew, shot forth from a wire on the tower above him, entered his head in that spot, and disappeared inside him, filling him from the top of his head to the soles of his feet with a white light, faintly blue along the edges.

Giant blue and white violets and pansies, so big they took up most of the sky and could be seen from inside the grounds, sprung up then all around on the horizon but R. York was no longer able to see them.

PAVAROTTI-AGAMEMNON

I. in the parlor

The tailor Pavarotti stood in the middle of the parlor of his three-room railcar (parlor, bedroom, kitchen) twelfth-floor apartment and looked outside. He was a big man, six foot two, with black curly hair thinning on top, a sparse, short matching beard, small round eyes spaced far apart and separated by a disproportionately delicate nose, a thin, perpetually twisted mouth, short neck, wide shoulders, big chest, bulging belly, knock-kneed legs, and huge feet. He wore a black suit, once well-fitting but now tight, white shirt with a wrinkled collar, and a thin, limp, black tie. On his feet he wore black patent leather shoes.

The shoes seemed to be firmly glued to the floor and when he had tried to move his feet a while back they wouldn't budge.

From the way they stuck to the floor it seemed they would never budge, no matter how hard he tried. The tailor Pavarotti was also unable to move the rest of his body, no matter which way he turned. Invisible threads, extremely strong, seemed to have been attached to every muscle, or rather fiber and even cell, of his body from the walls, ceiling, and floor of the room as well as, and especially so, the furniture in it, holding it firmly in place, similarly to, but much more than, the way threads had held Lemuel Gulliver when he found himself tied down to the ground on waking up the first morning in the land of Lilliput. As far as the furniture was concerned, it seemed to be its color that played the crucial role in its behavior: the liver-brown of the overstuffed sofa and armchairs and the bile-yellow of the doilies on the top of their backs where heads would rest—three, evenly spaced, on the sofa and one on each of the armchairs—as well as the similar yellow of the coffee table in front of the sofa and that of the big, old, stand-alone, cathedral-type radio. Strong partners in this were also the highly varnished yellow parquet floor and the imitation Persian, machine-made Karastan rug with an ill-defined red and brown pattern on a yellow background that covered most of the floor. The mirror on the wall above the fireplace directly behind the tailor Pavarotti was a dispassionate but attentive observer of what was going on.

There were two windows in the room with limp curtains hanging on them, once white but now pale gray from the many washings and the dust that had collected on them since the last one. The windows were of the guillotine type and were both raised high since it was the middle of summer and typically unbearably hot and humid. A trace of a breeze would occasionally find its way into the room and the left curtain on the window on the right had been blown outside where it clung to the rough brick wall. The tailor Pavarotti imagined it looking like the hand of a person clinging desperately to the wall so as not to fall down.

The tailor Pavarotti stood between the two windows, about six feet away from them, afraid to get closer because of the height. It was still early enough in the century that many people hadn't gotten used to tall buildings and suffered from this phobia.

It was Sunday morning but the city was already clogged with traffic. Through the right window the tailor Pavarotti could see down below in the streetcars standing still as he, one close to another. They were all black, with shiny sharp-edged bodies and looked like the number 4 repeated over and over with no end in sight. That is they seemed to be an infinitely long number 4444444.... The cars appeared to be part of a funeral procession but it looked as though they would never get to the cemetery and would remain standing where they were forever.

Through the window on the left the tailor Pavarotti saw the fourteen-story Acme building on the other side of the square. There was a clock at the top of its facade and a man dressed in a black tight-fitting suit was holding onto the minute hand while trying to get his legs over the hour one. His feet kept sliding on the face of the clock and he was unable to do this but kept trying over and over again. The clock showed quarter past nine.

There was no one else in the apartment and the radio, which stood directly behind the tailor Pavarotti under the mirror, blocking the fireplace, was turned on full blast. A tenor—the tailor Pavarotti didn't know who—was singing, holding the high C note for an inordinately long time, seemingly stuck in this the way the tailor Pavarotti was stuck in his shoes and the cars were stuck in the traffic in the street. The tailor Pavarotti could hear the windowpanes in the windows and the glasses way back in the kitchen being just on the verge of picking up the harmonics of the note and resonating with it. He hated to think what that would lead to.

2. in the sweat shop

It was noontime. The tailor Pavarotti was in his shop alone. All of his workers—four men, all young—had gone out to lunch. They had scattered to the small nearby parks to consume their sandwiches and drink an odd bottle of lemonade or root beer bought from a street vendor, trying to cool off in the shade under the trees. It was in the middle of July and unbearably hot, so being under a tree in a park hardly constituted cooling off, but was much better than staying on the top—eighth—floor of a building which is where the shop was located. As the owner, the tailor Pavarotti had to keep the place open in case a client happened to come in during his lunch hour or when one of his workers came back early. He trusted only himself with the key.

Lately concerned about his alarmingly growing weight he had consumed for lunch a lone orange and two glasses of water and was now resting in the chair, trying to regain his strength sapped by the hectic morning and heat. The skin of the orange, torn up into sharp pieces like shards from a clay pot, lay on the bottom of the nearby wastecan emitting a tantalizing scent, penetrating like an Italian tenor's voice—the only refreshing element in the dull heat weighing down on everything in the room. All the windows in the shop were raised high and although the air from the outside was free to come into the shop—it was a corner room—it made absolutely no difference—hot fetid air merely replaced hot fetid air. Unfinished work lay in dark heaps on the tables around which chairs stood abandoned in odd positions like dead bodies scattered on the ground, and pressing machines, with their upper boards raised high, resembled huge hippopotami with their mouths wide open, trying to cool off. The tailor Pavarotti, in shirtsleeves, slumped down in his uncomfortable wooden chair, his legs stretched out and his arms hanging down like sacks filled with sand, and gazed half-consciously at the opposite wall with its shelves of neat rolls of cloth and the front door in the middle of it. His sparse black hair stuck in curls to his sweaty skull as if glued in ringlets onto it and sweat stood out in big blisters on his chalk-white skin and formed huge dark stains under the armpits of his shirt.

Suddenly he saw the door in front of him open and a man come in. He was tall and thin, dressed in black, with a black top hat on his head, and carried a long thin package wrapped in brown paper under his arm. It looked like a very long hero sandwich. Unexpectedly full of energy the tailor Pavarotti jumped to his feet and rushed to the counter to welcome the potential customer. The man put the package down on the counter next to him and said he wanted to order a black suit of the formal cut to be ready as soon as possible—that afternoon or the next day. Taken aback, even a little frightened by the urgency, the tailor Pavarotti said it was certainly impossible to have the suit ready that afternoon and even the next day; the day after that however it could be ready—for a special price.

The price was no obstacle, the man said. He would settle for the day after the next one. How much would the suit cost?

It depended on the quality of the material and the person's size, the tailor Pavarotti answered.

He wanted material of the finest quality, the man said.

For a person of your size, the tailor Pavarotti said—he could judge how much cloth a person needed with no difficulty—the cost would be such and such, the rush surcharge included.

The suit was not for him, the man said, a smile spreading his thin lips like invisible fingers.

The tailor Pavarotti noticed then how really thin the man was—bones stuck out under the skin on his face and you could tell he carried no more flesh on his body under his clothes. His jacket and hat, he further observed, were unbelievably shabby, wrinkled, shapeless, and stained with white all over, as if the man had been rubbing against whitewashed walls or squeezing himself into corners, ashamed or afraid of being seen by people.

The person was bigger—heavier—the man explained. He would give him the dimensions.

The man then read off the dimensions for the tailor Pavarotti straight from his memory. Neck to floor the person was so many inches, he said. His back was that many wide, the arms that many long, the chest, waist, hip to floor, inseam that many, and so on, and so forth.

As soon as the man started talking, the tailor Pavarotti grabbed the pad and pencil he kept on the counter for such occasions and proceeded writing down the figures. The first one didn't evoke any reaction in him—it was just a number. The second one stirred something in his subconscious—there was something strange about it. With the third one he knew what it was—the dimensions were his own. He remembered them well. He gulped and felt hotter than heretofore. The fourth number came and it was as he had expected—another one of his. From that point on he kept writing the numbers down from memory, hearing with ever-increasing gloom how they were being echoed by the man's voice. By the time the man had finished he was drenched with sweat.

The man said nothing and the tailor Pavarotti knew it was his turn to act. He had to look at the man first. He raised his eyes and saw those of the man right in front of his. They were frightening—two black circles painted on white porcelain globes. There was no expression in them at all!

For an instant the tailor Pavarotti didn't know what to do but then the professional side of him took over—he was filling a customer's order and had to get on with it. Where was he? Oh yes, the cost.... He knew how much cloth he needed for himself. He calculated the new price and told it to the man.

That is fine, the man said and unexpectedly laid the money on top of the counter. He seemed to have held it in his hand. The tailor Pavarotti felt cold all over. Just by glancing at the bills, he could tell the amount was exactly right.

But he got a hold of himself again and said the person should come the next day for a fitting.

That wasn't necessary, the man replied, smiling.

The tailor Pavarotti noticed the man's teeth for the first time. They were very long and far apart like those in a skull. It seemed they could be easily pulled out by one's fingers. The idea was frightening and he felt the hair on his head stir.

Staring the tailor Pavarotti in the eyes with his frightening, empty gaze the man added he (the tailor Pavarotti) could try it on himself to make sure it fit. He grinned from ear to ear, the teeth in his mouth fully exposed for the tailor Pavarotti to see.

The tailor Pavarotti moved back as if away from something dangerous—an object that might explode—but remained standing in that spot, not knowing what to do. Luckily at that instant the man turned around, went to the door, and stepped out into the corridor.

Only then did the tailor Pavarotti notice that the man had left his package on the counter. He wanted to call to him to get the package but only a limp sound escaped from his mouth. The man was gone and the door slammed shut behind him.

As the tailor Pavarotti looked at the package he saw it had grown to a huge size. It was still wrapped in brown paper but no longer looked like a hero sandwich—more like a coffin. His face dripping with sweat, he tore the paper off and saw that underneath it there indeed was a coffin, one made from cardboard. He grabbed it and pressing it to his side as the man had done ran out from behind the counter, then to the door, and finally into the corridor.

It was long and narrow, with only the window in the far end illuminating it and reflecting on the shiny floor. The man was running down it toward the window with a female figure at his side, holding her hand. The woman—girl—wore a long white dress and a white veil on her head as if dressed for a wedding. The tailor Pavarotti realized it was his daughter Laura, recently deceased at the age of eighteen, and despair came over him. The weird man and his daughter were going to jump out the window!

Roaring like a wounded animal—a giant hippopotamus—the tailor Pavarotti shouted "Laura, Laura!" but the pair didn't stop. They were steps away from the window. He was going to lose his daughter in a matter of seconds!

At that instant he opened his eyes and saw one of his workers standing in the door staring wide-eyed at him.

3. on via veneto

A big café on Via Veneto in Rome. The cavernous interior spilling onto the sidewalk like guts from the belly of a huge slaughtered animal. Small, round, one-legged tables with white plastic-covered tops edged with metal. Next to them wrought iron chairs with no arms and round seats upholstered with red plastic. A movable iron barrier separating the café from the rest of the sidewalk. The tables, interior and exterior, 95% occupied. Similar cafés extending as far as the eye can see in both directions. Lava-like flow of people along the sidewalk likewise in both directions and a similar flow of cars in the street. The street wide. Its other side hard to see—hard not so much optically as psychologically.

Two men—a producer/director and his companion—sitting at one of the tables outside, next to the barrier. The producer/director in his fifties, the companion in his mid-thirties. Both handsome in an Italian way and fashionably dressed also in an Italian way. The producer/director has long wavy grayish hair, thick black-framed glasses, and strong features. His companion—short curly golden hair, gold-framed glasses, and fine features. There is something about him—perhaps all of the above and his long mobile fingers—that makes him seem a musician. The producer/director drinking a Perrier and his companion a Campari and soda. The conversation is carried on, naturally, in Italian.

The producer/director (*ending*): ...Agamemnon. I'd love to have Pavarotti do the role.

The companion waits for the producer/director to continue.

The producer/director (*continuing*): This huge body...powerful.... The trunk massive...straight up and down...with no waist...no room for finesse, esthetics...just strength...as if hued out of a giant tree trunk with an ax...in a hurry...just so there'd be lots of mass.... Powerful in its mass.... The arms and legs also crudely attached to the body...hanging down at the top and sticking out on the bottom...to support the trunk...that's all.... None of the bodybuilder's stuff...finely chiseled muscles.... They're actually not that big, I'm sure... not developed...like with most white men who don't do physical work and don't work out...but potentially powerful...powerful in reality too except not beautiful.... And on top of this giant, massive body this small head...like a normal person sticking out of it...out of this armor of flesh...a delicate person...hiding in this huge body to protect itself from the cruel world, his cruel fate.... And then those eyes...sad...always sad, even when he smiles or laughs...full of wisdom...sadness and wisdom...as if they know what's in store for them and all the rest that comes with it in the end.... Like a monkey's eyes...in a zoo...in a cage in a zoo...looking out sadly at the world, the people staring at them...knowing they belong to a monkey but unable to say it out loud...imprisoned behind the bars of the cage and of their monkeyhood.... And finally that mouth...thin and crooked with pain...turned down at the corners...sad and turned down at the corners even while smiling or laughing...always on the verge of trembling...like the mouth of a little boy who's about to cry....

The producer/director stops and pours himself some Perrier into the empty glass. The water argues with him from the bottom of the glass. It would have preferred to stay in the bottle. He drinks. Breathes with ease. His companion, imitating him, takes a sip of the menstrual liquid out of his glass and prepares to listen. No sign of disagreement on his face. He might not care what the producer/director says.

The producer/director (*fortified*): I don't know if he's hairy, but I'd make him hairy.... The chest and belly like a bear rug.... And the head too.... He's getting bald on top now, and I would give him a wig of thick, black, curly hair...sticking out in all directions...like in the ancient images of the sun...black curly rays framing his face.... The beard too.... The chest curly also... the curls also sticking out.... Down below a fistful, crotchful of hair...like darkness in a corner...with the little acorn of a penis sticking out of it like with some big white men.... Maybe only the testicles like a small clenched fist below supporting it...giving a pathetic little manhood salute.... When he'd be walking out of water the hair would cling to his body like a wet bathing suit...black, full, like in the old days.... The legs too...as if in black boots...black stockings...Roman or Greek buskins...like what the actors used to wear on the stage....

The producer/director takes another sip out of the glass. The water inside it has simmered down. The companion doesn't drink right away as if ashamed to be copying the producer/director. The latter stays quiet, thinking what to say next. His companion eventually sneaks in a drink. The producer/director then takes a drink himself not realizing he is imitating his companion. Empties the glass. Notices it but doesn't refill it. Leaves it for later.

The producer/director: The final scene.... It'd be in the desert with nothing but sand...but not dunes...barren land...and not golden but gray...like a vacant lot on the outskirts of Rome where boys play soccer...sand and gravel.... The palace a series of arches...single ones, in pairs and threes...not more...and no roof overhead, no ceiling...and some walls.... Except it's not a ruin but rather an unfinished structure...a work in progress that will never be finished.... Lots of arches and walls so that you have both emptiness and closeness...hemming in by emptiness...the principle of eastern, Arabic architecture...low and vast...like in the mosque, the cathedral in Cordoba.... The arches from granite...black granite.... In the center, almost up front so that you can see it well, a narrow enclosure, a bathroom.... Agamemnon has come home from his long journey and wants to wash off.... But there isn't any water.... Sand all around.... On the floor, the granite floor, sand scattered all over.... It hurts his bare feet.... He's naked...wants to take a shower...looks up.... Only the empty sky above.... Feels the sand under his feet.... Looks down.... Bends down and picks up a handful of sand.... Lets it flow out of his hand.... It flows in a meager current, some dust curling off from it.... He throws away the rest and puts his powerful arms out and presses with his hands against the two vertical walls hemming him in...trying to set himself free but it's clear it's in vain.... They're rough under his palms, the grains of granite digging themselves into his skin.... The black ones glittering like tiny pieces of obsidian.... He knows he'll not succeed.... He fills his lungs with air.... His nostrils flare.... The black curls shake angrily on his head and body.... He opens his mouth and emits a sound.... It's a scream and a song at the same time.... It undulates, rising all the time....

The producer/director pauses, being out of breath, pours himself more Perrier, the water this time protesting even more angrily—"Who does he think he is? And who the hell does he think *I* am?" He continues. The water simmers down, mollified by its outburst. His companion takes a sip out of his glass, once more waiting a moment so as not to imitate the producer/director.

The producer/director (*as if not having paused*): In the meantime, while this is happening, two figures appear behind Agamemnon. He doesn't hear them because he's making noise with his feet on the sand-covered floor at first and then because he's singing. But they tread stealthily anyway, on tiptoes. It's Clytemnestra and Aegisthus. She's tall and slender, with a classical face, but not beautiful.... The features like words describing her face as beautiful but not making it that.... A high forehead, thin eyebrows, a Roman nose.... Straight long hair framing the stony face.... Dressed in a burlap toga, carrying a bucket of sand.... Aegisthus also tall and slender.... A girlish figure.... Short curly golden hair.... Feminine features.... Dressed in a pink tunic that goes down only to the top of his thighs.... Tied with a golden rope.... The arms thin, round, like a girl's... pink.... Carries a huge two-edged ax made from obsidian in both his hands, pressing it to his chest because it's heavy.... It looks as though he loves it dearly.... Seeing Agamemnon the two stop for a moment...hesitate.... They'd perhaps expected something else or not thought the plan out completely.... Then Clytemnestra puts the bucket down, goes back behind the wall, and returns with a ladder. She puts it against the wall on the right, takes the bucket, and climbs to the top of the wall.... Aegisthus tries to keep it in place as much as he can while holding the ax.... She gets up on top of the wall...lifts the bucket high up...looks like a caryatid without a roof to support.... Aegisthus has let go of the ladder and raises the ax over Agamemnon's head.... Clytemnestra tips the bucket, pouring the sand over Agamemnon.... It's full of dust.... He's enveloped in it as if in hot, steamy water so that he's made almost invisible.... You can just see his legs and the outline of his body.... Aegisthus brings the ax down with all his might. Effeminate as he is he is still able to make it move fast, having gravity as a helper. It is a streak of black light...a black bolt out of the clear sky. The blade cuts the skin of Agamemnon's scalp just as his voice reaches its peak—a high...(*The producer/director turns to his companion for help.*) C?... B?...

The producer/director's companion (*without hesitation*): B is the norm for a good tenor, but the great ones hit C or even C-sharp.

The producer/director: C-sharp then.

He pauses, having forgotten where he was. Thinks for a while, then remembers and continues. His companion remains still throughout this.

The producer/director (*wrapping up*): At that instant too, from the complex of arches and walls, that is from the palace, on the left, a black figure detaches itself and seems to plan to run in the direction of the horizon.... Because the shape is so small it's hard to tell whether it's a female figure or the shadow of an arch that has somehow set itself free.... The composition looks like in the well-known picture by De Chirico.... But it clearly must be the shadow of a woman, probably that of Electra, because it's moving.... Cassandra must have already been

murdered by the perfidious couple somewhere in the thicket
of arches and walls…. There's no sign of Orestes however….
He's still a child and if the figure is Electra then she might
be taking him away to save him from being killed…. Isn't she
clutching something to her chest?… Or is there a shadow like
that of a small arch next to her?…

4. in the kitchen

In the kitchen of the tailor Pavarotti's apartment. The room
lit up by an overhead lamp with an adjustable enameled white
shade hanging low over the table in the center. The lower half
bright, the upper dark. A cozy atmosphere. It is in the daytime
and the reason for the light being on is because there is no window in the kitchen. Instead, it has a wall fan in one of the walls,
which at this time isn't turned on. The table rectangular, of the
butcher-block type, with tubular, chrome-plated chairs that have
woven straw backs and seats. All around cabinets of light wood
with glass doors and counters under them. (The place had been
remodeled recently at a considerable cost.) Lots of glassware on
the shelves inside the cabinets behind the glass doors. Along one
of the longer walls (the one with the fan) a modern gas stove
and a sink next to it, both white. A large modern refrigerator,
also white, in the right corner against the same wall. The place
messy—food and pots and pans on the counters, the table, and
the sink. (Both tailor Pavarotti and his wife work and there isn't
anyone to take care of the place.) The sink piled up high with
dirty dishes. Next to it a white dishrack full of dishes and pots
and pans that have been washed. An Italian coffeemaker purling
on the stove, indicating coffee will be ready soon. Two cups on
top of saucers next to the stove ready for the coffee.

The tailor Pavarotti and the producer/director sitting across the narrow side of the table from each other, the tailor Pavarotti with his back to the stove. Silence.

The tailor Pavarotti (*after taking a quick look at the stove*): The coffee will be ready soon....

The producer/director (*in a heavily accented but otherwise passable English*): Thank you.... It is an Italian coffee pot?

The tailor Pavarotti: Yes. It came from my grandmother. She made excellent coffee...like Italians do....

The producer/director (*lights up*): Oh yes! The Italians make wonderful coffee. I miss it.... I have not had a good cup of coffee since I left Italy.... Was your grandmother from Italy?

The tailor Pavarotti: Yes, both of my grandparents were born there...and my parents.... But I was born here.

The producer/director (*visibly intrigued*): Where was your family from?

The tailor Pavarotti: Campania.

The producer/director (*excited*): Really? What town?... My family is also from Campania.

The tailor Pavarotti: Cetara...a village on the coast near Amalfi.

The producer/director (*still more excited, leaning forward in his chair*): I know it.... I have driven through it.... My family is from Ravello.

The tailor Pavarotti: I've never been there.

The producer/director: And you have been to Cetara?

The tailor Pavarotti: Yes, as a kid. It's wonderful.... Packed all together between the road and the sea.... Delicious sea-food....

The producer/director: I know. It's all over the coast like that.

The tailor Pavarotti (*anxious to return to a topic he loves*): Even here my grandmother used to make seafood all the time.... My favorite was fish in scallop shells with rice...very simple.... Do you know it?

The producer/director: No.

The tailor Pavarotti: You can use any fish for it and you can mix different kinds of fish.... But it's best with a delicate fish like bass and some shellfish...shrimp or scallops.... But you use scallop shells regardless of what fish you have.... I think my grandmother brought them over from Italy.... They looked really old....

The producer/director remains silent, expecting the tailor Pavarotti to go on. He does so.

The tailor Pavarotti: You flake up the fish...fish you cooked before or leftover...and fry up some cooked rice with butter and grated Parmesan cheese.... You butter the shells and put a layer of rice and layer of fish and cover it with Béchamel sauce that has some egg stirred into it.... Then you sprinkle some more Parmesan cheese over the shells and put them in a hot oven for about ten minutes.... It's delicious....

The producer/director (*his eyes shining with excitement*): Sounds wonderful. I will try them myself.... I like to cook. (*After a brief pause.*) My grandmother was a wonderful cook too. There is one dish she made that I especially loved.... I make it all the time. It is...(*He hesitates, not knowing the word.*) animelle.... What do you call them in English?... Little soft things...from inside....

The tailor Pavarotti (*hesitates a little, then guesses*): Kidneys?

The producer/director (*firmly*): No, not kidneys.

The tailor Pavarotti: Liver?

The producer/director (*a little peeved*): No, not liver.... Two... round....

The tailor Pavarotti (*thinks he finally got it, his face lighting up*): Testicles?

The producer/director (*laughs*): No, not testicles!... You know...soft...the French eat them a lot.... Ris de veau....

The tailor Pavarotti (*doesn't speak French, so the phrase doesn't help him, strains, wants to say "Brains," prompted by the fact a brain has two halves, but dismisses it as certainly wrong, and in the end, sure it is wrong too, takes a wild guess*): Gallbladder?

The producer/director (*stumped at first, but in the end accepts the word, thinking all choices have been exhausted; the tailor Pavarotti is surprised his suggestion is accepted but also relieved his ordeal is over*): Yes, gallbladder...(*Hesitates for an instant but decides to ignore his doubt; clearly doesn't know what the words mean.*) I think.... (*Decides not to worry.*) Gallbladders cooked with peas.... You cook them in water and lemon juice first, then take off the skin and sauté them in butter.... Add some white wine.... Cook.... Add a little bit of flour and bouillon.... Separately you fry peas... fresh peas the best...in butter.... Add bouillon again and cook until tender.... Serve them with the gallbladders sprinkled with parsley.... With white wine...Pinot Grigio and Italian bread.... It is delicious!

The tailor Pavarotti (*amazed but also impressed; has never heard of gallbladder being eaten but explains it as rich people's food*): Sounds delicious...fancy.... My grandparents were simple.... My grandfather was a tailor.... And yours?

The producer/director: A lawyer.

The tailor Pavarotti (*smiles—he has suspected as much*): I thought so.... And your father too?

The producer/director (*smiles also, a little embarrassed*): Yes.

The tailor Pavarotti: And how come you're not?

The producer/director (*laughs heartily*): I am…. I studied law, but I liked directing better…. But being a lawyer has helped me as a producer…. (*After a pause.*) And your father was a tailor too?

The tailor Pavarotti: Yes…. He learned the trade from his father and I from him.

The coffeemaker makes sounds indicating the coffee is ready. The tailor Pavarotti gets up from the chair and goes to the stove.

The producer/director (*going back to the topic that has been on his mind all along*): So how about my offer?… As I said, I can't pay you any money but you will get a chance to express yourself artistically. That's the most important thing for a person…. To realize yourself…reach your potential…. I think you will be perfect in the role…. (*Adds as an afterthought.*) Besides you will grow as a person and ultimately will make a name for yourself…even after you are gone….

The tailor Pavarotti remains silent. Only the sound of coffee is heard being poured into a cup.

The producer/director (*presses on*): I take your silence as a sign of agreement.

There is a break in the sound of coffee being poured, then it resumes—it is poured in another cup. The tailor Pavarotti says nothing.

5. cassandra

Greek military camp near Troy. Peaked hulks of tents illuminated by enthusiastic torches merging in the distance with darkness. Sand trampled by many feet on the ground. A few sentries indistinguishable from torches and shadows they cause to be cast. A thin strip of white tide barely lapping the shore. The sea black as ink beyond that. It emits a smell like a sweaty armpit. An empty starless sky above.

Agamemnon walks in a determined step toward his tent. He is dressed in a leather outfit of the type you wear under your armor, sandals on his feet fastened with thin leather straps that crisscross his legs up to the knees, a stubby sword at his side. He has completed his duties as the commander of the Greeks and is hurrying to do what he has been thinking of all day—to possess his war prize Cassandra. He reaches the tent, opens the flap, bends down, and steps inside.

The tent is illuminated by a small bronze lamp standing on the floor next to the central pole supporting the tent. The flame is steady as a thin current of oil flowing out of a gently tipped amphora. Shadows are cast onto the sloping and vertical planes of coarse burlap-like cloth. They are steady too like fingers of a sure hand. Against the wall on the left, on the ground, lie in a heap on the ground his helmet, armor, and leg guards, like a hacked-up body of an enemy. The concave shape of his great shield has given up trying to hold all of them in. Against the wall on the right stands a wide, low, crudely made camp bed with the spread pulled down. A Persian rug almost completely covers the floor. Its irregular surface indicates there is sand underneath it.

Between the pole and the bed stands the slight, slender figure of Cassandra. She is turned partly toward the door as if not sure what to devote herself to—the bed or the door, in other words the former, or the person about to come in. Her hair is piled up high on her head like an amphora. It is magnified to a huge size in the shadow cast on the tent wall. The long black toga she wears makes her look taller—more stately and more fit for her role. A stream of words flows from her mouth like a thick current of oil from a fully tipped amphora. From the tone it seems she has been speaking for a long time and is not about to stop. Her speech, in Classical Greek, is full of "ai's" and "oi's" linked by "sh's."

Agamemnon is startled. He has expected Cassandra to resist him but not this way. He thought she would be defiant, ready to fight. He has heard of her love for tirades and takes what she does as her way of resisting. The words come fast and he can only make out some of them—"wife, lover, bath, ax, blood…." He knows she is a false prophet, pays no attention, steps up, and reaches out to undress her.

As soon as he touches her toga it falls in a heap at her feet like the covering cloth at the base of a statue being unveiled. He is startled and doesn't know what to do. She has untied it herself! She had resisted Apollo but will she give herself to him?

As soon as her toga falls off Cassandra stops talking, walks to the bed, lies down, and stretches out on her back. She has lain down in the middle of it and moves over to the far edge to make room for him.

Agamemnon is dumbfounded. She really is planning to give herself to him! He gulps and still doesn't know what to do. Naked, she looks like a boy, her ribcage pitifully narrow and her breasts like two swellings from bee stings. Only her hips and thighs are full, attesting to her femininity. And her pubic hair arrogantly sticks up in a black triangle over her pubic bone.

She is a woman, Agamemnon thinks, feeling his manhood struggling under his clothes. He has to undress!

Quickly his clothes fly off as if by themselves. They join the symbolic corpse in the corner on the ground. The last to go are the two sandals, which look like two-tailed comets with their leather straps streaking through the air.

Agamemnon is ready to join Cassandra but remembers the lamp. It will be better in the dark. Besides after having her he will want to go straight to sleep.

He walks over to the lamp, squats down, squashes the flame between his fingers like an insect, hears the wick crackle, gets up, goes to the bed, and lies down. It groans under his huge body, not sure it can support him.

Cassandra is still at his side. He can feel her fist like a rock between his body and hers. So that is what she is planning to do—not to fight him but not to be there...to let him have only her body....

He reaches out with his hand for her face and finds her lips. They are tightly pressed together like fingers in a fist. Her vagina too will be a fist he will have to squeeze into, he thinks. It doesn't matter—he will squeeze into it and possess her!

Her hair is spread over the bed, magnified in the darkness as on the tent wall earlier. He climbs on top of her and rests there—a mountain on top of a molehill. Surprisingly, her thighs spread under him to make it easier for him to enter, even if her legs don't rise up. He helps himself with his hand, enters her, and to his great surprise finds her moist inside. He finds her mouth with his, feels her lips part and then her teeth, letting his tongue in. What is going on? Does she really want him? Has she been waiting all day for him, thinking of this moment? She was half turned toward the bed when he came in....

He moves into her with no blockage. Does it mean she is no virgin...gave herself to Apollo after all or some Trojan goatherd, in the bushes outside the walls of Troy, on the dusty ground?...

No, there is a blockage, her body tenses up, she clutches his sides, then gives out a little sigh of pain carried on the current of her hot breath, and relaxes.

He plunges all the way into her and is in ecstasy. He has possessed her!

At that instant words start bubbling from under his mouth. She speaks again.

He lets her speak, moving back and forth in quest of his pleasure, the outline of which he can already sense.

Her voice is almost a whisper now but seems to be repeating the same words as before. Once again he hears "wife, lover, bath, ax, blood…," but now also other words, as well as phrases—"perfidious wife, effeminate lover, cousin, plot, bath, water, net or sheet, two-edged ax, bronze ax, blood, blood, blood…."

The words distract him from his pleasure, so he tries not to hear them, not to let them get in the way of his joy.

It gets stronger and stronger and he can feel strange things happening to her body. It moves in rhythm with his, even if barely noticeably, tenses up when his does, goes into a huge hard cramp, and when he bursts out in a series of loud cries, a little cry of ecstasy flies from her mouth too.

Immediately afterwards he hears her say clearly and calmly, "We will die together, you and I." He takes it to mean that she wants to be with him forever, die when he dies. He feels thankful and closes his arms tightly around her.

She goes on speaking however, making no sense, and he stops listening, rolls off her body (a dug-up mountain off a leveled molehill), lies still, and feels alone as if she weren't next to him. He hears the sea thumping down on the sand outside the tent some ten paces away, remembers his daughter Iphigenia he lost because of it, his country Argos which he left behind so many years ago that it is like a foreign land to him now, his wife who *is* a total stranger…. Thinks of the empty sky without end rising always higher and higher above him, above the tent…. Through the loosely woven cloth he can see torches flaming outside….

Through their crackling he has been hearing sounds of struggle coming from the nearby tent. He concludes it was Achilles' son Neoptolemus trying to claim his war prize Andromache. She was said to be exceptionally devoted to her dead husband Hector and must have been putting up a stiff fight. The sounds have stopped now. Has she won? Has Neoptolemus given up? No! New sounds appear. There is the tell-tale creaking of the bed and a breathy, reedy sound of a woman's rapid breathing. It is her, enjoying her new master! The sounds become faster and faster, louder and louder, and culminate in a series of unfettered female screams of joy—the faithful Andromache has begun begetting the first of the four sons she is still bound to bear!

6. on the beach

The tailor Pavarotti was walking out of the sea. After a hard day's work—shooting from sunrise till sundown—he had rushed to take a dip in the water to wash the sweat off his body and weariness off his soul. The sun had just set and the sky and the sea were the same oppressive industrial gray so that it was hard to tell where they met. The sea was flat as a table and there was no trace where the sun had set behind it as if it had wandered off in another direction. It seemed it might not come back in the morning.

Water clung to the tailor Pavarotti's body like glue, sticking to his shoulders, elbows, hips, seeming not to want to let him go as if claiming him as part of itself. It formed grotesque shapes the way it clung and in the end tore itself away so that he seemed a hideous sea creature trying to find its way onto the land.

His body hair stuck together in big patches like pieces of tattered black cloth clinging to his flesh—a badly tattered old-fashioned bathing suit. It merged around his hips with his skimpy black swimming trunks so that it was impossible to tell them apart.

Each time he lifted one of his legs it looked as if he were wearing on it a black buskin he had not bothered taking off with the rest of his costume while rushing to take a dip.

Before him lay the beach. It was low and narrow, composed of coarse gray sand that seemed mixed with cement. The flat landscape beyond it was partly obscured by the tall weeds. A chain-link fence in a bad state of repair teetered above them, further obscuring, albeit minimally, the view.

A long and low gray stucco structure with a flat roof that looked like a concentration camp barrack occupied much of the left side of the beach. It was there that the tailor Pavarotti and the rest of the crew were staying. There was no sign of any of them however—many, if not all, had gone off in cars to the nearby village—but next to the building on the left a fat middle-aged female figure swung energetically back and forth in a swing. The woman was dressed in a short black negligee that was too tight for her and had long and thick black hair that writhed in the wind like a ball of snakes. Her eyes were two black slits in her round face and in her wide-open mouth— open with joy at swinging—could be seen short rotten teeth with black spaces between them.

7. mycenae

In this dream the tailor Pavarotti is in Nauplion, which is close to Mycenae. He is in his hotel room that looks like a parlor. It has a fireplace and a bay window but there is no furniture in it. The tailor Pavarotti stands by the window and looks outside. The room is on the second floor and looks out on an intersection in which a few streets cross—more than two. The place is completely empty and brightly lit up like a stage set. The tailor Pavarotti is waiting for a taxi to pick him up and drive him to Mycenae where he is to take part in a performance. For a while there is no sign of the taxi but then it appears. It stops below the window, honks, and stands there with its engine running, smoke lingering around the tailpipe.

The tailor Pavarotti turns around and runs to the door. He is afraid the taxi might drive away. The fireplace is close to the door and as he passes it he notices an ax leaning against the mantelpiece. He is by the door already but he steps back, runs to the fireplace, and grabs the ax. He will need it for the performance.

He runs down the stairs and then through the brightly lit lobby into the street. The taxi is right in front of him, he opens the back door, gets inside, shuts the door, and leans back in the seat. The taxi lunges forward, drives screeching around the intersection, and proceeds down one of the streets. The tailor Pavarotti doesn't tell the driver where to go because the latter knows that already.

The streets are all brightly lit, still like a stage set, and completely deserted. It is late at night. They drive for a while and then stop alongside a large building without windows, built like a warehouse. They have arrived. The tailor Pavarotti feels this even though Mycenae is a fair distance away from Nauplion in reality and looks completely unlike the building. He pays the driver, steps out of the cab, shuts the door, and heads for the building. He has left the ax in the taxi and doesn't remember it for the rest of the dream.

Inside, the building is dimly lit but looks like a vast stage full of props and people. The atmosphere is hushed as if before a performance and everyone is busy doing something, clearly knowing what their task is. The tailor Pavarotti also seems to know what he is to do for he confidently wends his way past the people through the labyrinth of objects, curtains, and partitions. He comes to an area that looks like a kitchen in an old farmhouse or perhaps a castle. Against one of its walls there stands a huge fireplace looking like a small stage. A fire is burning in it under a giant cauldron suspended on a hook, its sides black with soot. It has obviously been used for cooking for many years. A woman wearing a long peasant dress with a white apron and a similarly white kerchief on her head is busy stirring the water in the cauldron with a huge wooden spoon. She stands with her back to him but he sees enough of her to know he has never seen her before. Steam rises from the cauldron indicating the water is about to boil. A wooden stool stands on one side of the fireplace with a big white sheet folded on top of it. The tailor Pavarotti knows in the performance he is supposed to take a bath in the cauldron and on stepping out of it he will be dried by the woman with the sheet.

There is a huge rectangular wooden table in the middle of the kitchen with chairs around it. A few men are seated at its far end playing cards. The tailor Pavarotti doesn't go up to the woman as one would expect but to the table and sits down on the chair in the center of it facing the fireplace. Apparently he will wait there until the woman calls him—when the water is ready. It is supposed to boil before he gets into it. He seems to feel it is normal to bathe in boiling water and is not concerned about it. He leans back in the chair and waits to be called to play his role.

The men playing the cards get rowdy. Something unusual must have happened and they laugh, slap each other's backs, and shout. They speak in English, which doesn't surprise the tailor Pavarotti. He waits patiently, observing what is going on. So far no one has paid any attention to him as if he were invisible.

At one point another person appears in the kitchen—a young-ish man with short, curly black hair and black-rimmed glasses, dressed in tight gray or blue pants and a checkered shirt with rolled-up sleeves. The tailor Pavarotti hasn't seen him come in and it is possible that the man has been there all along but that he merely hasn't noticed him. He observes that he also has never seen the man before. The man putters around the kitchen doing some chores and from time to time exchanges words with the woman. They apparently work together. The tailor Pavarotti doesn't hear what the two are saying. They speak too softly for that. Then at one point the man puts his arm around the woman and gives her a hug. She squeezes up against him in response indicating the relationship between them is intimate. It must be so for at one point the young man leans over and kisses the woman on the mouth. She appears to laugh in response—the tailor Pavarotti isn't sure because she still has her back turned to him as when he stepped into the kitchen.

Time goes on and at one point the tailor Pavarotti notices he hasn't seen the young man for a while. He must have gone out of the kitchen to do something. At that instant he feels a sharp pain in the nape of his neck penetrating all the way to his Adam's apple—he has been skewered by something sharp. At the same time a pair of strong hands press him to the back of the chair and tie his neck to it. He is now impaled on something like a knitting needle that goes through the high back of the chair and is tied to it. Although his arms and legs are free he can't move. He explains to himself that this is because he is dead. This doesn't frighten or surprise him and he accepts it. Apparently he has expected it. He then hears loud words behind his back, right over his head, saying: "He's ready now." It is the young man speaking. It is he who has killed him. This again doesn't trouble or surprise him.

The woman turns around and looks in his direction. Her black eyes in the middle of her white face look like bullet holes on a target sheet. Although the woman's face has features like all normal faces, and although the tailor Pavarotti sees them, they don't register in his mind with the effect that to him her face is blank like a target sheet. The woman seems to be looking at a spot above him—clearly the man standing over him. She doesn't seem to consider him—the tailor Pavarotti—important to look at. As she does this she wipes her hands on her apron. She replies that they will put him—the tailor Pavarotti—into the water shortly. The water is in fact boiling already, vigorously at that—thick steam rises from the cauldron and from time to time it splashes up into the air.

The woman goes away from the fireplace and is busy doing something else. There is no sound coming from the man behind the tailor Pavarotti's back and he seems to have gone away again. The tailor Pavarotti waits patiently for what they will do to him. He can follow pretty well what is going on in the kitchen by moving his eyes. Another outburst of sound comes from the men playing cards. The tailor Pavarotti shifts his eyes to see what has happened there and sees they are laughing and slapping each other's backs as on the previous occasion. Life goes on as if nothing had happened.

8. in the kitchen again

The tailor Pavarotti's kitchen, the same as before except the light above the table has been replaced by a neon light on the ceiling. It is very bright, so that it would cause a person with sensitive eyes to squint. You can't miss a speck of dust in it. Because of this the place looks even messier than before but in fact is less so—the counter on the right has been cleaned up a little to make room for preparing food. The tailor Pavarotti's wife Luciana and his cousin Morton Goldberg (his Italian father's sister married a Jewish man) are fixing a supper of freshly made basil and tomato sauce and pasta—linguini, also freshly made. The two are busy at the counter and stove, the tailor Pavarotti is relaxing on the comfortable tubular chair on the other side of the table. He is drinking a Perrier straight out of the bottle, the other two are sharing a glass of Chianti whenever their tasks permit it and when they remember. The kitchen fan is on, providing an appropriately monotonous, mechanical background music to the action.

The tailor Pavarotti's wife a voluptuous Italian beauty with a body like a mound of steaming pasta under a thin, skimpy dress. The tailor Pavarotti has often voraciously partaken of it, frequently at lunch time. A massive, assive, soft-brass ass. Tits to match with two hard nipples like metal buttons managing to nearly work their way through the sleazy fabric. Long, black curls swooning, abandoning themselves to gravity. Soft brown eyes assuring of more softness inside. The tailor Pavarotti's cousin tall and slender, has his father's curly golden hair, which is cut short, and wears gold-framed glasses. Dressed in tight jeans and a black silk shirt with long sleeves, temporarily rolled up. Delicate features and likewise delicate movements, the latter making some people suspect him of being a homosexual. (The tailor Pavarotti sometimes affectionately, sometimes less so, calls him a "faggot," to which the cousin invariably responds with an ambiguous laugh.)

The tailor Pavarotti (*after sipping from the bottle, his voice changed temporarily*): When is the damn sauce going to be ready?

The tailor Pavarotti's cousin: Soon, soon…. (*After a pause.*) Those tomatoes and basil you brought were really fresh…. Where did you get them?

The tailor Pavarotti: From a cart vendor in the district….

The tailor Pavarotti's wife (*her interest perked up*): A cart vendor?… Really?… I didn't know they're still around.

The tailor Pavarotti (*sipping from the bottle again*): I was surprised too…. I haven't seen one for ages…. Looked Italian too…not Mexican…. (*Changes the subject, hearing the pot on the stove start making noise.*) Haven't you put in the pasta yet?… The water's boiling.

The tailor Pavarotti's wife (*fluffing up the huge pile of pasta on the board in front of her while sprinkling it with flour*): I'm about to…. Have to get it ready…. What's the hurry?… Haven't you had anything to eat today?

The tailor Pavarotti (*miffed, mimics her*): What's the hurry…. I've been sitting here for an hour…. I'm hungry.

The tailor Pavarotti's cousin goes over from the stove where he has been mixing the sauce to the tailor Pavarotti's wife's other side and takes a sip out of the wine glass. He is close to the tailor Pavarotti's wife and while doing that puts his left hand on her behind. Massages it gently.

The tailor Pavarotti (*exploding*): Take your fucking hand off her ass, you faggot! Get yourself a woman of your own! You're forty now and you still don't have anybody!

The tailor Pavarotti's cousin (*laughing, while continuing to massage the tailor Pavarotti's wife's behind*): If I'm a faggot, you've got nothing to worry about….

The tailor Pavarotti (*livid*): Luciana, how can you let him do it?!

The tailor Pavarotti's wife (*wiggling her behind from under the tailor Pavarotti's cousin's hand*): Cut it out, Mort.... (*He takes his hand off her. She speaks to her husband.*) What's this jealousy all of a sudden? He's been doing it for years....

The tailor Pavarotti's cousin (*turns to face the tailor Pavarotti, laughs*): The hunger brings it out in him.

The tailor Pavarotti's wife is ready with the pasta, picks up the board and brings it over to the pot with boiling water. Steam rises from it like smoke from Vesuvius.

The tailor Pavarotti's wife (*to the tailor Pavarotti's cousin*): Come and help me.

The tailor Pavarotti's cousin comes up to the stove, offers the tailor Pavarotti's wife the glass, she sips from it, he puts the glass on the counter next to the stove, then helps her with the pasta. With his delicate fingers he picks it up in bunches and drops it in the boiling water. It is as if he were touching strings on a harp. The tailor Pavarotti relaxes. He has been mollified by the actions. Takes a sip out of the bottle.

Pasta safely in its place, the tailor Pavarotti's wife goes back to the counter and starts cleaning up. The tailor Pavarotti's cousin starts mixing his pot of tomato sauce.

The tailor Pavarotti's cousin: Smells wonderful.... Reminds me of Tyler's [*the tailor Pavarotti's first name*] bile sauce....

The tailor Pavarotti's wife (*fearing trouble*): Leave him alone, Mort! He didn't know what *animelle* meant....

The tailor Pavarotti: But you liked it when we found out it was sweetbreads, didn't you?

The tailor Pavarotti's cousin (*laughing*): Christ! You didn't even know what sweetbreads meant in English!... I don't believe it!...

The tailor Pavarotti (*laughs in turn*): Ha, ha, ha!... I thought you ate them at Christmas...in mincemeat pie.... Didn't you ever...as a child...think that sweetbreads were the same as sweetmeats?...

9. the other pavarotti

The tailor Pavarotti stood in the middle of the parlor of his apartment and sang. He stood about nine feet away from the windows, facing them, his right leg pressed against the outer right corner of the coffee table. It dug itself into his flesh just below the knee, causing him discomfort, but he wasn't aware of it, being fully engrossed in his singing. It was Sunday morning, middle of summer and typically unbearably hot and humid. Because of this both windows in the room were raised high to let in fresh air but there was no breeze and the curtains hung limp on them as if forever unable to move.

There was no one else in the apartment and the radio in the room was turned on full blast, tuned to a station over which an opera was being broadcast. It was Puccini's *Tosca,* one of the tailor Pavarotti's favorite operas, with the other Pavarotti, Luciano, the tailor Pavarotti's favorite opera singer, in the role of Cavaradossi. The tailor Pavarotti had been listening to the opera virtually from the beginning, standing, again virtually all the time, in the same spot. As the opera drew to a close, when the other Pavarotti was singing the aria *"E lucevan le stelle,"* the tailor Pavarotti's favorite opera aria of all, and his voice rose to the highest pitch in the phrase *"amo la vita, tanto la vita,"* the tailor Pavarotti, without any previous plan or desire to do such a thing, opened his mouth and emitted a sound that to him at least seemed exactly the same in pitch and volume as that of the other Pavarotti. He was dumbstruck when he did this but continued holding the note. The other Pavarotti went on singing as he was supposed to but the tailor Pavarotti was no longer aware of him. He was fully absorbed in himself, in the sound he was making. He realized that he was singing the note without any difficulty and that if he wanted to he could go higher—a full octave higher. He decided to do this, did it, and again felt as before—that he was singing the note without any difficulty and that if he wanted to he could go up another octave. Once again he did this and once again had a feeling he could go another octave higher but at that instant heard a loud, low—ugly, as he felt, in comparison with the sound he was making—noise. For an instant he didn't know what it was but then noticed there was no sound coming out of the radio and realized what had happened—he had popped one of its tubes with his voice! Dumbfounded, not knowing what to do, he continued holding the note and heard another two or three similar noises, indicating more tubes popping in the radio. Almost simultaneously he heard a loud melodious sound coming from the left window—a pane shattering and falling to the floor, then an identical sound from the right window—another pane breaking; then, after a fraction of a second, a much louder but similar sound from behind his back—the mirror over the fireplace shattering and coming down in a cascade of sound; and finally a whole Niagara of noise from the depth of the apartment—a total annihilation of his wife's carefully assembled collection of glassware in the kitchen.

Chills ran up the tailor Pavarotti's spine and hair stood up on his head. What had he done?! If he didn't stop singing God knows how much more damage he might do!

Instantly he stopped singing but the frightening sounds continued resounding in his memory as real as echoes. He was drenched with sweat from head to toes. He had created a real mess!

The first thing that came to his mind was the radio. It was a memento from his grandparents on his father's side, one of his favorite possessions. How was he going to fix it? Last time he had to replace a tube, which was a number of years ago, he had to go through unbelievable contortions to find it. Now it was three or four tubes, or perhaps more, and a few years later. Who knows if tubes were still being made? And then there were the two windowpanes, and the mirror, and what was sure to be a total disaster in the kitchen…. Did he break anything else?

He remembered the clock on top of the Acme building across the street. Did he break the glass on its face too? For an instant his heart sank, for that would be one more thing of which he was guilty, but then he decided he couldn't have done it. The clock was surely too far away. Then he relaxed completely. He was being silly. Way back then he saw that man cling to the hand on the clock…. There was no glass over it!

10. the murder

On the way to the studio the tailor Pavarotti stopped off at a hardware store to pick up an ax, which was going to be used in the performance. He was asked to do it. It was to be a two-edged ax such as is used for felling trees and he was lucky the store carried it. He got the last one. He felt uncomfortable carrying the ax in the streets and on the subway however and wanted to buy a lumberjack's jacket to put on so as to look like a lumberjack but the hardware store naturally didn't carry any. They directed him to an army-and-navy store a few blocks away and he was overjoyed to find that they did carry such jackets. He got one—in a red and black square pattern, which was exactly what he wanted. He put it on and proudly strutted out of the store carrying the huge ax on his shoulder. In the subway he kept it between his feet as he held onto the bar while the train sped along, and nobody seemed to find anything strange about him. As always the train was packed with people and everyone was engrossed in his or her own thoughts.

As always too the studio was teeming with people going about their business and the tailor Pavarotti had to wend his way past them through the labyrinth of objects, curtains, and partitions to where he was told to show up. The final scene was to be patterned on the murder of Marat by Charlotte Corday, in particular as depicted in the painting by David. He had gone to a bookstore and studied the picture carefully so that he knew what to expect.

After getting lost a few times he found the spot the performance was to take place in and was surprised at how it looked.

It was way in the back of the studio, in a corner behind partitions, curtains, ropes hanging down from the ceiling, and all sorts of equipment piled up high in stacks. He was under the impression that there were going to be spectators witnessing the performance but that didn't seem to be the case. The few chairs that stood in a row in one spot must have been either left over from some other event or were designed for people participating in the performance to rest on. It was possible though that the performance would be watched on closed-circuit television piped into an auditorium. There were four more chairs standing in another spot on the set but they were definitely not for spectators. A string quartet was supposed to accompany the performance and the chairs were obviously reserved for them—a violin or viola case sat on top of one of them and next to another one—the rightmost—a cello case lay on the floor.

Signs that things were being readied were there however—a high-backed zinc bathtub stood in the middle of the set on top of a wooden pallet, such as is used for storing heavy objects in warehouses to be easily moved by lift trucks. A big white bedsheet was spread out in it, and some water had already been poured into it and could be seen on the bottom; it had made almost the whole sheet wet. The water was warm, for as the tailor Pavarotti bent down over the bathtub he felt warmth rising from it as from a freshly slept-in bed. He verified this by sticking his fingers in the water. The bathtub was going to be filled to the proper level so that it would cover his body to his waist. Next to the bathtub stood a coarsely made low wooden table, probably nailed together from spare pieces of wood that lay around the studio. It stood at an odd angle to the bathtub apparently placed there only temporarily. It would be moved next to the bathtub later and presumably covered with a cloth. Beside the bathtub on the ground stood a white porcelain pitcher from which he was supposed to pour water over his head to wash off the soap. The former was still empty and the latter nowhere to be seen. The sheet which hung down over the back of the bathtub would be thrown over his head, and he would be struck with the ax from behind—he was not told by which of the two conspirators.

Not knowing what to do with the ax, the tailor Pavarotti leaned it against the bathtub next to the pitcher. Ultimately someone would turn up to take care of it. He felt strange in the lumberjack's jacket but didn't know where to put it. Laying it down next to the ax didn't seem appropriate, so for the time being he decided to leave it on. Besides he felt a little cold. He hoped the water would still be warm when he got into the bathtub.

Feeling lost he looked around but as he expected he saw no one. Where was everyone, he wondered. He was sure the performance hadn't been canceled. He would have been one of the first to be notified if that were the case. He assumed people were merely busy with their tasks somewhere else and eventually would turn up. That was undoubtedly true of the producer/director—he was always on the phone calling people up. But what about his wife Luciana and cousin Morton Goldberg? Why weren't they there? He concluded that they were probably wandering about the studio having gotten lost as he had done.

But all of a sudden the situation changed. A person appeared on the set—the cellist. He was handsome, tall and slender, with delicate features and short, curly golden hair, was dressed in street clothes—an elegant suit probably of Italian cut—and wore gold-framed glasses. Not paying attention to the tailor Pavarotti he went up to the cello case, opened it, took out the cello, put the case back on the floor behind the chair, sat down on the chair, and started strumming the instrument to see if it was tuned. Then footsteps were heard behind the curtains or partitions coming nearer as well as people's voices. Things were starting to move.

SURGERY

1. the surgery candidate

As the surgery candidate's car turns into the neighborhood where the doctor's office is located the atmosphere changes from a sunny late Monday afternoon to that of a gloomy early Sunday morning. The streets are deserted, empty of cars and people, with everyone still in bed sleeping out the last drops of fatigue acquired during the usual grueling workweek and a hectic Saturday spent shopping. Clouds—grayness with no visible delineation—hang low over the rangy single-storied homes separated from the street by dense hedges of giant arborvitae bushes. There are no sidewalks. The broad, smoothly paved, and immaculately clean streets curve this way and that as if swaying in a slow solo dance, passing equally broad, smoothly paved, and immaculately clean driveways, either empty—cars hidden behind doors in garages—or displaying expensive foreign models with slothful, obese bodies.

The surgery candidate has been given detailed instructions for getting to the doctor's office—he has written them down on a sheet of paper which he holds in his right hand while keeping his left one on the steering wheel—and he is following them by casting a quick glance at the sheet of paper from time to time while driving along. The neighborhood looks completely unlike those in which doctor's offices are normally located and the surgery candidate has had a feeling since entering it that he has gotten lost but time and time again the instructions on the sheet are borne out by the landmarks—street names, stop signs, numbers of blocks and the like—and he has to make an effort to suppress his doubts and to follow what the words on the sheet of paper tell him to do.

Finally it appears that the surgery candidate has arrived at the place of his destination—such and such a house on a particular side of such and such a street after such and such an intersection. The building is sheltered from view by the usual requisite dense wall of closely growing giant arborvitae bushes and he cannot verify if the building is in fact the correct one. His doubts having been proven wrong so many times, however, the surgery candidate suppresses them, stops the car by the curb, shuts it off, picks up the large yellow envelope with the MRI pictures the referring doctor had ordered, lying on the seat next to him, puts the sheet with driving instructions in its place, gets out, locks the door, and walks to the driveway up ahead. Once in it he relaxes—a sign next to it displays the correct number and under it another sign proclaims on one line "dr. kax" and below it "surgery"—exactly what it should, the terseness implying competence and lowercase letters a degree of esthetic flair.

The house behind the sign at the crest of the gently domed lawn looks completely unlike what the surgery candidate expected. It is single-storied, low and rangy, molding itself along the curving land like a rug thrown over it—clearly a residential home rather than a professional building—and momentarily the surgery candidate has again a feeling he has made a mistake as he has had many times getting here. The sign, however, like a stern voice of authority reminds him this is reality and he suppresses the emerging doubt and resolutely marches along the gracefully curving concrete path that leads from the driveway to the house, clutching the envelope with the MRI pictures in his hand while pressing it passionately against his side like something dear to him, for instance his child. He comes to the conclusion the doctor practices out of his home, something that, although rare, is not unheard of. The heels of his shoes make sharp loud sounds on the concrete and the shock of each impact is propagated up his legs toward his pelvis where it dissipates as in a fog.

The house has a vaguely oriental appearance. In addition to being low it has wide overhanging eaves, which remind the surgery candidate of the work of Frank Lloyd Wright. He concludes the architect of the building must have been influenced by that architect. The association with a renowned name, one esteemed by him to some degree to boot, relaxes the surgery candidate and the gloomy mood that has been with him ever since he got into the car practically disappears in him similarly to the way the shocks projected up his legs from his heels do this when they reach his pelvis. The surgery candidate comes to the door, sees a small white rectangular button next to it, and pushes on it. A timid tremulous sound is heard inside the house and almost instantly a deep buzzing noise follows it like that made by a bumblebee in distress. It is the door being opened. The surgery candidate was not asked to identify himself, so he is expected.

This pleases the surgery candidate; he puts his hand on the doorknob, the door obediently yields, he steps inside, and shuts the door behind him.

For an instant he is stunned by the darkness that envelops him as if by a blinding light. He expected the usual brightly lit reception room in a doctor's office but the space is illuminated only by the light coming from the outside through the bank of tall windows on the right covered with nearly closed venetian blinds. As his eyes get used to the darkness—a matter of a fraction of a second—he is surprised once again. Before him in the spacious, almost empty room paneled in dark brown wood, stands an unusually tall, curved reception desk made out of silvery metal with a flower vase full of giant white gladioli in the center. On the wall directly behind it hangs a round electric clock with a silvery face similar in color to the desk and with thin straight hands but no numbers on it. There is no sound in the room and no sign of anybody and the surgery candidate has a sudden wish to turn around and rush outside as soon as he can. He is again afraid he hasn't come to the right place or if he has he would rather not be there. At that instant, however, he hears a human voice coming from somewhere saying something. It is metallic sounding with a drone-like quality similar to that a damaged audio speaker would make and a thought crosses the surgery candidate's mind that it is a machine speaking to him in place of a receptionist. He realizes then the voice has said he can proceed to the examination room and at that instant notices something stirring behind the vase. It is the head of a woman, clearly the receptionist. She has spoken to him. He walks toward the desk and looks at the woman. She is in her thirties, with thick platinum hair combed smoothly down over her forehead, on the sides, and in the back, cut off evenly at the bottom so that it looks like a helmet, with narrow eyes and an oval face, wearing a tight-fitting blouse or dress made out of a silvery material that seems to be designed to match the metal in the desk and the clock. This is all he can see of her because of the height of the desk. The woman repeats what she said before, namely that he can proceed straight to the examination room.

Flustered, the surgery candidate stops and tells the woman his name. She replies coldly she knows that, that he is expected, and that the doctor will see him shortly. The surgery candidate is about to move but remembers the pictures he is holding. He tells the woman he has brought them along. She replies it is fine. He can show them to the doctor.

This is obvious and the surgery candidate turns hot with shame, and although there seems to be only one way for him to go—to his left into the hallway—he asks discretely if this is where he should go. Still like a machine the woman replies that that is right.

Wet with sweat the surgery candidate turns left and without saying anything walks. He notices then the floor under his feet is
soft and sees it is covered with a gray industrial grade carpeting.
It spreads before him into the hallway as if carrying him along.

The hallway is paneled with the same dark brown wood as the
reception room and has a low ceiling. There seem to be no
doors in it on either side and the surgery candidate has a feeling
he is in a culvert under a railroad track or a highway. He has an
urge to bend down but stops himself for obvious reasons and
merely strides along, his footsteps muffled by the thick carpet.
He comes to the end of the hallway and finds himself in a very
large open space that appears to be part of a penta- or a hexa-
gon, with ground-to-ceiling windows in the walls on his right,
its floor sunken on two separate levels below the level of the
hallway. A sunken garden with dwarf trees, clusters of reeds,
carefully arranged and interestingly shaped rocks, pebbles, and
neatly raked sand lies outside the windows. The surgery candidate comes to the edge of the step and stops.

The higher level that stretches to his right seems to be the dining room, with a very long rectangular wooden table and high-
backed matching chairs arranged around it, and the lower one
before him the living space, with a giant L-shaped gray leather
sofa, a number of matching armchairs and ottomans, and coffee and end tables distributed among them. The floor is covered on both levels with the same gray industrial level carpeting as in the reception room and the hallway except that in the
living space a good portion of it is replaced with white marble
in the shape of a giant kidney. There is something vaguely oriental and reminiscent of Frank Lloyd Wright about the nature

of the space and the decor in it and the sunken garden outside
the windows adds to this impression. It seems an extension of
the inside of the house.

Calmed by the sight and the association with a name he knows
and respects, seeing the sofa down below, the surgery candidate quickly walks down the two steps, comes up to the sofa,
and sits down on it. He automatically puts the envelope next to
him on the left but then, as if that were a mistake, quickly picks
it up and puts it down on his lap. He obviously has a strong
need to be in close contact with it. He sits from then on in this
position without moving, his knees pressed together, staring
into the space before him.

2. dr. kax

The surgery candidate sits for what seems to him like ages but
is in reality merely minutes and then hears a sound coming
from the hallway. It carries with it a sense of strain, even suf-
fering, and at the same time of great ugliness, evoking a feeling of pity mixed with disgust. Startled, the surgery candidate
straightens up on the sofa and focuses his eyes on the space
before him.

Moving down the hallway in his direction is a frightening
creature, some five feet tall with a huge elongated shiny head,
broad shoulders, thin spindly appendages up front and wide
limp ones behind. It moves down the hallway slowly, throwing
its body from side to side like a giant seal traveling along the
beach.

The surgery candidate is overcome by fear, he tenses up, ready to stand up and defend himself or run, and at that instant sees the creature lift its head, revealing a likewise huge face with giant shiny eyes and a mouth twisted in an excruciating exertion, full of huge white teeth, even like piano keys.

Now the surgery candidate has no strength to stand up and only a bubble of a scream forms itself in his lungs but it grows limp and deflates as he realizes it is a crippled man moving toward him with the help of a pair of canes with T-shaped handles while dragging his paralyzed legs along. He is dressed in a short white coat with a white shirt and a dark tie underneath and a pair of baggy gray pants too long for him so that they hide his feet. The man wears gold-framed glasses and is completely bald, with a strangely-shaped head—bulging up front and in the back and sunken in the middle like a giant peanut. He breathes heavily, sucking the air in through his nostrils and clenched teeth and pushing it back out the same way while staring fixedly at the surgery candidate—clearly his goal which he is determined to reach at all cost.

Although still frightened, the surgery candidate settles back on the sofa and waits for the man to come. The latter reaches the edge of the step at the top, puts the cane in the right hand down on the step below, then the one in the left one, carefully brings his feet down, repeats this process on the next step, and proceeds moving toward the surgery candidate. Having moved a few steps he lunges to the right so fast the surgery candidate is about to let out a scream again, thinking the man is falling and will hurt himself, but the latter twists his body so that it lands on the little ottoman that stands there and makes himself comfortable on it. He has clearly done this on purpose and the bubble of a scream grows limp and deflates again in the surgery candidate's lungs before it has time to get out.

Once on the ottoman the man takes the cane he held in his left hand into his right and holding both of the canes in it propels himself with them toward the surgery candidate—the ottoman has wheels on its legs and moves easily since it stands on the marble-covered part of the floor.

The surgery candidate then comes to several realizations at once. The man is the doctor he has come to see—Dr. Kax. The room is where the doctor sees his patients. Being paralyzed he moves on the ottoman. And the floor is covered with marble to permit the ottoman to move easily.

The ottoman stops so close to the surgery candidate that it nearly touches his knees and the doctor twists his body toward him and extends his head so that his face is no more than two feet away. He stares the surgery candidate in the eyes and the latter has a feeling the doctor is inside his head. He finds the sensation very uncomfortable, as if he were reading from too close up, and tries to move his head back but is unable to do it. He has already moved it as far back as possible. The doctor's eyes are very clear behind the lenses like pebbles on the bottom of a mountain brook but the surgery candidate observes he cannot tell if they are brown or gray. He also realizes he cannot tell the doctor's racial origin. His skin is brown so that he could be from one of the southern countries—India for instance—but he could also be a European—for instance a Pole—with a good tan. This leaves the surgery candidate in a state of suspension.

The following conversation takes place between the surgery candidate and the doctor.

The doctor (*skewering the surgery candidate with his gaze; his speech is accented but the surgery candidate is unable to guess the origin of the accent; thinks it might be an affectation*): You are in great pain?

The surgery candidate (*momentarily feeling more uncomfortable, tries to move his head back but as before is unable to do it; trembling with fear*): Nnooo...nnot always...just sometimes...especially in the evening, when I go to bed....

The doctor (*without a pause, like a cat pouncing on a mouse*): When you're in bed lying down or before?

The surgery candidate (*calmed down, relaxing*): Before.... The pain usually goes away when I lie down.... It's usually gone when I wake up in the morning.... (*Quickly corrects himself, afraid of being caught lying.*) Essentially always.

The doctor (*pressing on, as if not caring what the surgery candidate has said*): How long do you have the pain?

The surgery candidate: You mean during the day?... It depends.... It's usually not there when I'm resting.

The doctor: No, the symptoms—when did they start?

The surgery candidate (*blushing, apologetic*): Oh, I'm sorry.... About six months ago.... (*Once again afraid of not telling the truth.*) Five and a half.

The doctor: You've had therapy? How long?

The surgery candidate: Six weeks.

The doctor: With no improvement?

The surgery candidate: No.

The doctor (*smiling; the surgery candidate notices the side of the doctor's head heave as if there were no bone underneath the skin; is startled; thinks of the side of a dachshund moving while the animal breathes; imagines the side of the doctor's head to be hot and soft like a dachshund's stomach*): It was to be expected.

The surgery candidate says nothing, feeling downcast, convinced of his inadequacy. The association of the doctor's head with the body of a dachshund is gone from his mind, replaced by concern about his situation.

The doctor (*for the first time in a lively, almost cheerful voice*): You see, your case is very much advanced. (*Kinder, explaining himself.*) I saw you walking down the hallway. (*The surgery candidate realizes there must be a peephole or a one-way mirror in the hallway through which the doctor watches his patients; thinks it is clever; is impressed by the doctor; realizes he has been impressed by him from the beginning.*) It's clear what's wrong with you.

The surgery candidate feels more ashamed of his inadequacy but feels he can do nothing about it. Suddenly he sees a ray of hope.

The surgery candidate (*sitting up, lively*): Dr. Kac…. (*He is referring to the physician who has sent him.*)

The doctor (*interrupting, knowing what the surgery candidate will say*): Dr. Kac has told me everything about you.

The surgery candidate (*clinging to his hope*): He thinks….

The doctor (*has anticipated this too*): He thinks there is a chance you might not need surgery, but also that you might need it. That's why he has sent you to me, to make an evaluation. But think for yourself…. You've been very conservative so far. You've waited six months, had six weeks of therapy, and have not gotten better….

The surgery candidate (*glad he can finally agree with the doctor, not realizing the connotation of what he will say*): No, actually worse….

The doctor (*smiles; the side of his head heaves again like that of a dachshund; the surgery candidate remembers his previous association; feels sick at the thought of the doctor's brain hot and soft under the skin like a dog's stomach*): There you are. You've actually gotten worse. So what choice do you have? You either have surgery or you live like you are.

The surgery candidate feels hot all over. Sweat stands out on his face. He swallows hard. The idea of living in his present state is utterly unacceptable to him. His whole being revolts against it. The feeling is similar to retching.

The surgery candidate (*vehemently*): No, I can't go on living like this.

The doctor (*quietly*): It's your choice. So you will have surgery.

The surgery candidate feels the heat subsiding in his body. He relaxes and adopts a more comfortable position on the sofa. Breathes more deeply.

The surgery candidate (*feeling really close to the doctor*): But do you think the operation will help?

The doctor (*less friendly, more professional*): You never know. These procedures are about ninety-five percent effective.

The surgery candidate (*completely dispassionate, as if talking about abstract data*): Meaning that ninety-five percent of patients are cured?

The doctor: That is correct.

The surgery candidate: And they are fully recovered?

The doctor: Between ninety and one hundred percent.

The surgery candidate: You mean they are ninety to one hundred percent better?

The doctor: That is right.

The surgery candidate: And are there any adverse effects?

The doctor: Some ten percent are worse off than before.

The surgery candidate (*turning hot all over again and sitting up; incredulous*): Ten percent?

The doctor: Ten percent of the five percent who don't get better. That is half a percent of the total. You have one chance in two hundred of getting worse.

The surgery candidate (*somewhat relieved*): And can you have then another operation?... To correct the problem?

The doctor: We don't have a way of rectifying that right now. You would have to live with the pain from then on.

The surgery candidate (*feels wet under his collar; runs his finger along it*): Wow!... That's bad....

The doctor: But you have a choice. You don't have to go through with the procedure.

The surgery candidate sits still, not knowing what to say—he has already made his choice. Then a question pops up in his mind.

The surgery candidate (*relieved he can ask something*): So what sort of things would you do in my case?

The doctor (*livens up, sits up straighter; looks the surgery candidate in the eyes*): I don't know. I have to open you up first.

The surgery candidate feels sick at the words "open you up." For an instant he thinks he might faint but the sensation goes away. Then he thinks of something that might help.

The surgery candidate (*hopeful again*): I have some MRI pictures here.... Dr. Kac had ordered them. Wouldn't they tell
you something?... (*He picks up the envelope lying in his lap to offer
it to the doctor.*)

A shadow of a smile passes over the doctor's lips. He leans
forward to take the envelope. The cuff of his shirt comes out
of the sleeve of the coat. It is immaculately white and stiff
with starch, held together by a large gold cufflink in the shape
of a surgeon's scalpel.

The sight of it shocks the surgery candidate like electricity. He
then notices the doctor's fingers. They are long and powerful
like those of a pianist. The doctor's thumb looks especially im-
pressive, its base muscular like a big chicken thigh. The surgery
candidate has an image of a big chicken thigh in a puddle of
dark sauce lying on a plate. He is thinking of *coq au vin* which
he had a number of times and which he likes. He pushes this
image out of his mind however and thinks about the doctor's
thumb. He concludes the thumb is most likely so strong because of the doctor's deformity—the weakness of his legs. As
is invariably the case in such situations other parts of the person's body develop more strongly than in normal people. The
strength of the doctor's hands, the surgery candidate further
observes, probably attests to the former's being a good surgeon. Surgeons undoubtedly need strong hands. He remembers the lavish praise his referring doctor had heaped on this
one. Lastly the surgery candidate observes there might be a
connection between the doctor's teeth being so healthy and the
weakness of his legs—bones in other parts of his body might
be healthier as a consequence.

The doctor takes the envelope being handed to him.

The doctor (*dismissive*): Pictures don't tell you much. Just that there is a problem and where it lies. It's only once you're inside the patient that you see what's wrong. It's the details that count. A little physical difference may have profound consequences.

Still he has been influenced by what the surgery candidate has done for he propels himself with the help of the canes toward the window and stops at it. He takes a few of the pictures out of the envelope and expertly throws them against the window making them stick under the frames. The windows appear to have been designed in such a way that they could hold pictures in place.

The surgery candidate sees white shapes on the black background in the pictures like outlines of a complex system of underground tunnels. A warm feeling for them springs up in his heart as if for something closely connected with him, for instance his child. He also feels pride at them being so complicated as he would at seeing his child excelling at something.

The doctor looks at the pictures and then speaks.

The doctor: Yes. Just as I thought. There's nothing new here for me. There's a growth here, and here, and here, as is to be expected. (*He points to different spots on different pictures. The surgery candidate can't see them from afar, thinks of getting up and going to the doctor but decides not to. He knows he has lost the battle.*) But there are all sorts of different things in reality. I won't see them until I'm inside you.

The last phrase doesn't have the same shocking effect on the surgery candidate as the previous similar one did. He has gotten used to the notion.

The doctor puts the pictures in the envelope and propels himself back to the surgery candidate—a spot a little farther away from him than before. He extends the envelope to the surgery candidate.

The doctor (*indifferently*): You probably want to get a second opinion so you should take these. The other doctor will want to see them.

The surgery candidate (*frightened, blushing, confused; afraid he might offend the doctor if he agrees; takes the envelope nevertheless*): Nnooo.... I....

The doctor (*insistent*): You should. You must have some doubts. This is not a trivial procedure and you shouldn't just take my word for it.

The surgery candidate (*blushing more, holding the envelope up in the air, where he took it from the doctor*): I.... You.... I....

The doctor says nothing however, turns away from the surgery candidate, and propels himself toward the window where he was before. Slowly, as if picking up a bunch of loose things, he raises himself off the ottoman, stands supported on the canes, moves closer to the window, and looks outside. He seems to be examining the garden like the MRI pictures before.

The surgery candidate is in a state of shock. He doesn't understand what has happened—has he offended the doctor in some way? He feels guilty although he doesn't know why. He wishes the doctor would turn around and speak to him. It is clear he won't do this however. The interview has ended. He must leave.

With his face burning hot and his mind empty, pressing the envelope with the useless MRI pictures to his chest, the surgery candidate turns away and walks to the hallway leading out of the room.

3. dr. kax's wife

Silence once again reigns in the room. The doctor stands still, leaning on the canes and examining the garden. No noise penetrates into the house from the outside.

Then a faint sound like the crackling of a sheet of mylar barely touched by fingers is heard coming from the hallway, gradually growing stronger. Someone is again walking down it into the open space. Soon a figure appears in the doorway—a tall slender woman dressed in a long tight-fitting silvery dress with low-heeled matching slippers on her feet. Her thick straight platinum blond hair is combed down on all sides and cut straight across the forehead, around the sides, and in the back, forming a helmet reminiscent of those used in space travel. Her face is oval and eyes narrow and she looks very much like the receptionist but in fact she is not the receptionist but the doctor's wife.

The woman comes up to the edge of the steps, stops, shifts her body onto one leg as if leaning on a railing (there isn't one there), and speaks to her husband.

The doctor's wife (*timidly*): Can I speak to you for a minute?

The doctor has heard his wife and is turning toward her as she speaks to him.

The doctor: Yes, what is it?

The doctor's wife (*stepping down and moving to the edge of the next step*): I'm going out shopping and wanted to make up the menu for the whole week.... What do you want to have?

The doctor throws himself down onto the ottoman and with the help of the two canes in his right hand, as he had done before, propels himself toward his wife.

She steps down and sits on the step with her feet apart, leaning forward.

The doctor propels himself further and stops a couple of feet away from her. He makes himself comfortable on the ottoman leaning back and supporting himself on the canes which he again holds in his right hand.

The doctor's wife (*after her husband has settled down*): You said you wanted to have meat loaf.... Do you want it tonight?

The doctor (*after a brief pause*): Yes, that will be fine.

The doctor's wife: Then what about the rest of the week?

The doctor (*relaxed*): This is what?... Monday?...

The doctor's wife (*softly*): Yes.

The doctor leans back on the ottoman and supports himself on his left arm. He then lifts the canes, brings their tips over to the edge of his wife's dress, and lifts it up. It rises obediently to the level of her knees. The doctor pushes it back a little so that it exposes the space between her legs. He looks into it, narrowing his eyes, and sees the darkness that has collected there in a mysterious triangle. He rests the elbow of his right hand on his thigh to make it easier for him to hold his arm up and stays in this position until the end of the conversation.

The doctor (*after deliberating for a while, his attention divided between thinking and looking*): So meat loaf and mashed potatoes on Monday, risotto with mushrooms and cheese Tuesday, Welsh rabbit [*a dish of toasted bread and melted cheese over it*] on Wednesday, tandoori chicken and pulao [*Indian dishes, the second one a sort of pilaf*] on Thursday, bigos [*a Polish stew of sauerkraut, kielbasa, tomatoes, carrots, and potatoes*] on Friday, salmon with sautéed potatoes on Saturday, and....

The doctor's wife (*interrupting*): Saturday we're going to the Kacs'.... I forgot to tell you.... We've been invited.

The doctor (*unperturbed*): Oh, OK. Then salmon and sautéed potatoes on Sunday. (*Thinks very briefly.*) And the vegetables as always, what goes right with the dishes.

The doctor's wife: OK.

The doctor (*pushing the edge of his wife's dress a little farther back and peering in more intensely; the view doesn't change much however*): I don't know if you remember all that. You don't have anything to write it down with.

The doctor's wife: I think I have it.

The doctor (*as if not having heard his wife's words*): I'll give it to you in alphabetical order. This way you'll remember it better.

His wife says nothing, with no sign of annoyance.

The doctor (*rattling off*): 1. bigos, 2. meat loaf, 3. risotto, 4. salmon, 5. tandoori chicken and pulao, 6. Welsh rabbit. Have you got it?

The doctor's wife (*obediently rattling off herself*): Bigos, meat loaf, risotto, salmon, tandoori, Welsh rabbit....

The doctor (*satisfied*): OK.

Feeling the conversation is ending the doctor takes the canes away from his wife's dress and sits up, resting again on the canes in his right hand.

His wife pushes the dress down so that it covers her legs. She prepares to rise.

The doctor (*stirring on the ottoman*): Is that friend of the Kacs' going to be there?... The mountain climber.... He gives me the woollies when he talks about going up cliffs.

The doctor's wife (*screws up her face, puzzled*): The woollies?...

The doctor (*impatient*): Yes, you know.... The creepy-crawlies... hairy ones....

The doctor's wife (*still unsure, thinks, then speaks*): You mean caterpillars?...

The doctor (*glad she finally got it*): Yes,...that give you goose bumps when they crawl over you.

The doctor's wife (*smiles, finally understands her husband*): Oh, you mean "the willies...." He gives you the willies.... That's different.... It doesn't have anything to do with creepy-crawlies.

The doctor (*surprised but not upset*): It doesn't? I didn't know that. "The willies" then. He gives me the willies.

The doctor's wife (*goes back to his question*): No, I don't think he's going to be there.... It'll be just us and them.

The doctor: That's good. It'll be quieter. It looks like I'll have a rough week this week. I'll be worn out by Saturday. (*Pauses. Then thinks of something else.*) I forgot.... Get a fresh bunch of gladioluses. The ones in the vase don't look good.

The doctor's wife (*senses the conversation is coming to an end; rises*): Alright.

The doctor (*thinks of another topic that has apparently been on his mind*): How is Beatrice [*their daughter*] doing with her skating lessons?

The doctor's wife (*was going to turn away but stops; the topic is of interest to her too*): Fine.... She loves them.... Wants to take more...on Saturdays....

The doctor (*pleased*): Good. Let her. Maybe one day she'll win an Olympic gold medal. (*Laughs.*) It'll go with my collection of gold cufflinks.

His wife says nothing and merely smiles a non-Mona Lisa smile.

4. dr. kax's dream

The roof above the ice skating rink is like a starlit sky. There are electric lights in it and they twinkle like stars. The place must be ventilated from the roof for freshness streams down from above onto the ice as from the sky on a summer night. He breathes in the air and his chest seems about to burst with it and with joy.

He stands with his hand on the railing running along the edge of the ice and on the other side of it, right next to him, stands the kind of stool he sits on while operating, with wheels on its legs. His skates are slippery under him, their blades moving back and forth like horses anxious to take off. He has to hold onto the railing so as not to let them carry him away. Then he decides to skate. The rink is a huge circle or oval with the ice lit up from below like a swimming pool at night. The sight is beautiful. There may be other skaters on the ice but if this is so there are few of them and they are far away. Compared to the vast size of the rink they are nothing.

He lets go of the railing, moves his right foot forward, and takes off. It is as if he were propelled by a silent jet attached to his back. He is flying along the ice. Afraid of falling he puts his left foot down on the ice and propels himself with it. Now he is really flying. The movements of his legs are effortless and he is fully in command so that there isn't any danger of his falling down. He decides to try something new—to make a circle. He whirls around like a stone in a sling and flies even faster forward. Joy once more builds up inside his chest making it seem about to burst. To make sure this doesn't happen he breathes out. His breath sounds like a short laugh. He knows now he can do all sorts of things—he moves from side to side, spins, jumps, and whirls in the air. The mastery he has over his movements is incredible. He feels he could do anything he wanted—even jump up and touch the roof way up above which is really the sky. Without planning to do this he realizes he is spelling his name out on the ice. He looks and sees written in beautiful cursive letters cut out on the ice the words "dr. kax"—all in lowercase the way he likes it.

He doesn't have time to gloat over something he has already done—he skates on, spinning, pirouetting, whirling, and so forth.

Then he decides to speed up. Everything is a big blur. The new experience is even more exhilarating. He slows down and then speeds up again moving in this fashion along the ice rink. When he tries to stop he has to turn his skates sideways and they produce a shower of ice that flies from under the blades. It is like water coming out of a garden hose when you press down on it with your thumb. It feels nice. He tries it a few times.

He is moving fast again in a straight line and sees a wall of green plants on his right like a field of sugarcane. They grow out of the ice as if from soil. He wants to see if he can cut the plants down with the blades of his skates. He puts his feet one after the other in a straight line, tilts left, and moves along the line of the plants. They fly out from under the blades like the shower of ice before. The feeling is wonderful. The line of plants is long but he moves along it to the end and turns back. He has mowed down a whole wall of plants, which have fallen in a neat row, lying along the edge like a bunch of children put down to sleep. They are green and white like giant gladioli.

A narrow lane has been left open between the mowed down plants and the next row that still stands up. He liked cutting down the plants so much he decides to do it again. He moves back some distance, skates as fast as he can, puts his feet in the same position as before except he leans the other way, and runs down the narrow lane mowing the plants down as before. They fall obediently down as he moves along them to the end.

Having mowed down this row he decides to do the same with the next one and repeats the process. Then he does the same a few more times. Now a long field of plants lies obediently on the ice but there are still a lot left standing up. In fact he cannot see the end of the plants.

Suddenly he notices something stirring among the stalks about in the middle of the wall standing up. It seems to be a person who is trying to hide—run away from him. This upsets him. He cannot let this happen. He speeds down the narrow lane, this time not mowing the plants down, and stops where the plants had stirred. They are pushed to the side and even broken in places, a sign someone had moved through them. As he looks closer he can see a dark figure moving through the plants away from him, about to disappear. He again feels he cannot let this happen and rushes in among the plants in pursuit of the person. The figure is tall and thin, gangly, obviously a man. He will not let him get away!

The plants grow close together and are sturdy so that it is hard for him to break through them but he pushes forward with all his might. He must succeed! He pushes the plants apart with his hands and legs and tramples them down with the skates. He is making progress.

The man up ahead is making progress too so he must press on hard not to let him get away. The man is desperate and therefore isn't making as much progress as he could. He thrashes about with his arms and legs, his feet get caught on the plants, and he nearly falls down. Because of this he himself is gaining steadily on the man. The latter must hear him because his actions get more frantic and therefore even less effective. A few times he actually falls down but manages to get up quickly.

He presses on calmly and resolutely however and now is some ten feet behind the man. Hearing him right behind his back the latter glances around while running. His face is a picture of despair—flushed, with round eyes and wide-open mouth. It is framed with wet disheveled hair.

Not seeing where he is running, the man falls down. He tries to get up but is unable to do this. In a few seconds he himself is right over the man. The man knows this, rolls over on his back, and looks at him in despair. The man's face is the same as before—a picture of despair—and he—the man—reaches out with his hands up begging for mercy. The man's belly is defenseless before him like that of a dog begging for mercy from a stronger dog that has beaten it in a fight.

He stands for a brief moment not knowing what to do. Then he remembers the blades on his skates and how they mowed down the plants. In an instant he knows what he will do. He lifts his right foot and puts it on the man's belly. Then he has a better idea and moves it higher up, in the middle of the man's chest. He has to move his left foot forward to do this.

Now he presses down hard on the man's chest with his foot and moves it back and forth a few times. After a few moves he hears a cracking noise and his foot sinks in. It is as if he had split open a watermelon with the blade of his skate. He looks down and sees he has parted the man's chest and it has opened up like a watermelon split down the middle. The blade of his skate is deep inside the man's chest. It is surrounded by something soft and pink—the lungs. The man's face is still—the features relaxed, the mouth wide open, and only whites showing through the crack between the eyelids. He is dead.

He takes his foot off the man and sees the inside of the chest fully. There are the lungs, but also the windpipe and esophagus, and on the right something round, throbbing. It is the man's heart. He isn't quite dead yet!

He bends down and grabs the heart with his hand. It is warm and resists him as if electric current were passing through it.

5. the surgery candidate's dream

He is standing at the side of an ice skating rink holding onto the railing, afraid of falling down. He is on skates and doesn't know how to skate so he is unsteady on his feet. Every time he lets go of the railing his feet move under him and he is about to fall down. The rink is empty except for one person—a man—skating in the distance. It is Dr. Kax. He is an excellent skater, a real pro, but apparently more of a speed skater than a figure skater, for he skates in a circle around the edge of the rink and moves very fast.

Here comes the doctor and flies past him. The man comes very close, almost touching him, which scares him because he is so unsteady on his feet. He nearly falls down. Terrified, he holds onto the railing with all his might while his feet do a pathetic little dance under him.

He watches the doctor skate and can't help feeling admiration for the man, about how fast he moves. Every movement of his body is perfect and propels him forward along the ice.

Only a few seconds have elapsed and the doctor comes by again and this time bumps into him. Now he actually starts falling but manages to stop himself from hitting the ice by holding onto the railing. When he steadies himself and is standing up again he searches anxiously with his eyes for the doctor afraid that what had just happened might be repeated. The doctor is speeding like a bullet along the edge of the rink leaving behind a gray streak. Now he is coming toward him. From the way he is looking at him it is certain his aim is to hit him. This time he is going to knock him down. He is doing it on purpose!

He decides to flee. He would like to get off the ice into the stands but there is no opening in the railing. The green carpeting on the steps and among the seats looks so inviting but there is no way he can get up there.

Then he notices a thicket of tall green and white plants like giant gladioli growing out of the ice along one side of the rink not far away. He can hide there. Forgetting about the danger of falling down he decides to do it. He can make it there before the doctor gets to him. He runs on the sides of his skates, tilting his feet out so that they don't slide under him, and soon reaches the plants. He can hear the doctor behind him wheezing and the blades of his skates hissing on the ice.

He is in among the plants now and tries to get as far between them as possible. He spreads them with his hands and tramples them down with his feet. They tower over him like sugarcane.

There are sounds coming from behind him telling him he is being pursued by the doctor. He is terrified and runs as fast as he can but is unable to move very fast because of the plants. He falls on his knees a few times but manages to get up and run.

But the doctor is gaining on him. He can hear the man coming closer and closer. His actions get more and more frantic and finally he falls face down on the ice. The plants hem him in on all sides and he can't get up.

In despair and with a plea for mercy he turns over on his back offering himself to the doctor like a weaker dog beaten by a stronger one in a fight. He sees the doctor above him with his giant face, huge round eyes behind the thick glasses, the mouth open, and teeth huge and shiny like piano keys.

The doctor lifts his right foot and puts it on his chest. He feels the hard blade of the skate press down on him and then his ribcage parts like a watermelon cut open with a knife. His ribs stick up like fingers pleading for mercy with his innards red between them.

He faints and then comes to again. He appears to be dead but still can see things. He feels no pain however.

The doctor is bending over him and pulls something out of his inside with a pair of drumsticks, one in each hand. It is something long, thin, and white. He thinks it is his entrails but the doctor puts it in his mouth. It appears to be spaghetti.

He is in a restaurant, used as a dish from which the doctor is eating using the drumsticks as chopsticks, one in each hand. He thinks that being dead isn't such a terrible thing after all.

6. dr. kax's daughter

On a frozen pond, a public place, in the middle of what seems to be a sunken garden, vaguely Japanese in nature. Late winter or early spring afternoon with the tips of tree branches swollen into buds ready to burst like fingertips bulging with blood. They seem to be in pain as fingers swollen with blood would. Late afternoon, cold, slanting sunshine. The colors brown and gray except for the bluish-white ice and sky.

The surgery candidate and Dr. Kax's daughter Beatrice standing on the ice facing each other, neither of them aware of the other's identity. His gangly figure as if blurred in the dark baggy street clothes, her graceful one in a red skating outfit sharply outlined. Both on skates—he a novice, unsteady on his feet, she a near pro, unaware of them as if they were part of her. No one around in the immediate vicinity and no sound of anyone else coming from anywhere. It is possible they are the only ones on the pond.

The two have just collided through his incompetence. He fell down and has gotten up with her help. At first he was massaging his right wrist, on which he had landed, but he has stopped that now, feeling his pain has gone away. After the obligatory "I'm sorry's," "It's my fault's," and "No, no, it's mine's," they have started to talk.

Dr. Kax's daughter (*in response to his typical conversation starter*): Beatrice. (*Pronounces it as "BEE-triss."*)

The surgery candidate (*intrigued*): Spelled "b-e-a-t-r-i-c-e?"

Dr. Kax's daughter (*vivaciously*): Yes…. (*Points to the ice where her name is spelled out in lower-case letters.*) See…I've spelled it out…. I had just done it when we collided.

The surgery candidate (*looks in amazement*): It's fantastic…beautiful…. You're a real pro.

Dr. Kax's daughter (*not overly excited, apparently used to such praises*): That's why I didn't see you…. I was too absorbed in what I was doing.

The surgery candidate (*eager to get back to the previous subject*): But your name should be pronounced "Beh-ah-TREE-chey…." It's an Italian name.

Dr. Kax's daughter: Really? I thought it was Dutch.

The surgery candidate: No, Italian for sure. They pronounce the "c" as a "ch" before the high front vowels "e" and "i."

Dr. Kax's daughter (*incredulous*): But the queen of Holland is called "Beetriss"…. I was named after her…. My father went to school in Holland.

The surgery candidate: Oh, her name is pronounced "BEH-ah-treex…" spelled "b-e-a-t-r-i-x." It's derived from Beatrice but the original is Italian.

The girl remains silent, clearly not ready to argue. He continues his lecture, obviously very interested in the subject.

The surgery candidate: The name spread all over Europe…. It was made famous by the great Italian poet Dante….

Dr. Kax's daughter (*interrupting, glad to be able to do this*): I've heard of him….

The surgery candidate (*as if not having heard her*): He wrote about her…. He met her when she was young…fourteen I think…. Is that your age?

Dr. Kax's daughter (*quickly*): Yes. (*Corrects herself.*) Thirteen and a half.

The surgery candidate (*anxious to return to the main topic*): She was walking down the street in Florence…with her mother or a chaperone I think…and he saw her…. He never forgot her after that…. Wrote a whole book about her…. *La Vita Nuova*…. *New Life*…. And then mentioned her again in his great work, the poem *The Divine Comedy*.

Dr. Kax's daughter (*again interrupting, but less forcefully this time*): I've heard of it too….

The surgery candidate (*again ignoring the interruption*): He talks about her in the section called "Paradise…." But I think she comes up first in "Purgatory…." Dressed in red…. (*Laughs.*) Like you are.

Dr. Kax's daughter laughs too but has nothing to say.

The surgery candidate: I have a beautiful edition of the work… illustrated by the famous French artist Daumier…. (*The girl doesn't interrupt him this time—she hasn't heard of the artist.*) I could show it to you. (*Changes the tone of his voice.*) Would you like to see it?

Dr. Kax's daughter (*eagerly*): Yes. (*After some hesitation.*) Sure….

The surgery candidate: Do you come here often?

Dr. Kax's daughter: Sometimes…when I can…. I usually skate at a closed arena but I prefer the open air.

The surgery candidate: Yes…it's much nicer…. (*Silence. He realizes he should go on.*) So when will you come here next?

Dr. Kax's daughter: I don't know…. The weather's getting warm…. I don't know if I'll come here again this season.

The surgery candidate (*visibly troubled*): Oh, don't worry…. It won't get that warm right away…. Are you going to come next week?

Dr. Kax's daughter (*after thinking a little*): Yes, maybe….

The surgery candidate: When?… The same day?

Dr. Kax's daughter: Yes…on Wednesday…. I get out of school early on Wednesday.

The surgery candidate (*joyful*): Great. I'll bring the book then.

Massages his wrist again which he realizes has been hurting all along after all. The girl notices this.

Dr. Kax's daughter (*concerned*): Does it hurt?

The surgery candidate: Yes...a little.... It seems to be getting worse....

Dr. Kax's daughter: You should go to a hospital.... Or see a doctor.... (*Remembers.*) My father is a doctor...surgeon.... You can see him.

The surgery candidate (*genuinely intrigued, stops massaging the wrist even though it continues hurting*): Really?

Dr. Kax's daughter: Would you like to see him?

The surgery candidate (*hesitates at first but then gives in enthusiastically*): I.... Well.... I think so.... Yes!

7. first second opinion

In the office of the doctor from whom the surgery candidate has come to seek a second opinion. A high-ceilinged room (twelve feet high?) in what looks like an old building, with tall windows (three) and doors (two), its walls painted a surgical green; the ceiling and woodwork white. The floor uneven, covered with an off-white (but clean) linoleum, light shining on it because of the irregularities in its surface looking like shallow puddles of water left after washing. A big old-fashioned gray metal desk some five feet away from the wall, facing away from it, its top covered with papers. Two of the windows in the wall behind the desk and the third one in the wall on the left. The windows curtainless. A full-sized human skeleton (real?) suspended on a wire on a stand in the corner by the window. White metal cabinets with glass fronts against the wall on the right, with models (specimen?) of human skeletal structure and glass jars with real human body parts preserved in alcohol on the shelves in them. Facing the desk, against the opposite wall, a huge gray metal cabinet where the doctor keeps his patient records, with stuff (mostly additional records) piled up on top of it almost to the ceiling. A roughly four-foot high stepladder next to it. The two doors on both sides of the cabinet, both shut. The surgery candidate and the doctor huddled together behind the desk.

The doctor old (seventy? more?), tall (six-two? -three?), with chalk-white skin and jet-black hair (dyed for sure) slicked over the completely bald top. The white chalk skull contrasts brutally with the jet-black hair along the edge up front and where it shines through. A bristly walrus mustache (lighter color than the hair—not dyed?) covering a repaired harelip (repaired quite well). The voice typically for people with a cleft palate hollow as if coming out of a barrel. Very cross-eyed. The eyes brown, scarily penetrating like spinning electric drills. His right leg artificial all the way up to the hip. Sits with it sticking out under the desk. The surgery candidate on his right, uncomfortable on the chair because of the doctor's artificial leg.

The two are looking over pictures of the insides of people the doctor has taken himself. He is an amateur photographer and judging from the pictures a pretty good one.

A rapport was established between the surgery candidate and the doctor from the moment the former stepped into the office and it has grown progressively stronger during the consultation. At one point in the middle of the consultation, apparently when he felt the rapport had reached the proper level, the doctor asked the surgery candidate to get some records for him which were somewhere on top of the cabinet. It was hard for him to get up there with his artificial leg and the receptionist (his assistant) had left early on personal business. (The surgery candidate had been let in by the doctor himself.) The records had clearly been on his mind and he apparently was afraid he might forget to ask the surgery candidate to get them before the latter left. The doctor inquired if the surgery candidate was up to getting up on the stepladder but the latter assured him he was. He was glad to be able to assure the doctor of this—felt this might convince the latter there was no need for his having an operation. The doctor pulled the stepladder over to the front of the cabinet, the surgery candidate got up on top of it, had to climb on top of the cabinet, searched among the folders and bundles there (some of them seemed to contain dried long-stalked flowers), found the desired records, gave them to the doctor, got down, and put the stepladder in its place. The consultation resumed after that but it was soon thereafter that the doctor had offered to show the surgery candidate the pictures and had invited him to bring his chair over next to his. By then the two were like two chums who had known each other since childhood.

At this moment the two have been looking at the pictures for some five minutes. The consultation will presumably resume when this is over. The pictures are big, mostly 8 1/2 x 11, glossy, in vivid, shocking colors.

The doctor (*flipping over the picture they have been looking at and revealing the next one; it shows the open abdomen of a patient, the skin held apart by metal clamps*): What beauty!... A veritable flowerbed.... Peonies, roses, tulips, gladioli.... A secret garden you've entered which is yours to explore.... It's helpless...can't move...but it trusts you...wants you to get to know it.... (*Changes the tone of his voice.*) There's no better way to get to know a man than to operate on him...get inside his body.... That's the closest sort of intimacy there is.... (*Points to a shiny gray shape.*) That's a stomach.... Now watch it open up. (*Flips the picture over and refers to the one underneath it showing a pale pinkish-beige cavity, all empty, with rounded walls like a basin.*) See it?... What beauty!... (*The surgery candidate agrees but is too overwhelmed to say anything.*) And how it trusts you!... Even more than before!... It offers you its very center, its most vulnerable part...most beautiful one... the most secret part of the secret garden...a spot behind a bush.... (*Quietly flips this picture over, and then the next few, and stops at one with a big red-brown object of irregular shape, so that it is hard for it to be compared to anything.*) And this is a liver.... Gorgeous!... Like a giant orchid with floppy petals...with one big petal.... You almost want to bury your face in it.... And bones.... (*A pause. Flips a few pictures farther to a photograph of a thigh bone deep between two big muscles being pulled apart by metal clamps.*) Look at this femur.... What whiteness!... Blinding!... There isn't even any blood on it.... It rejects it like a saint a sin.... Immaculate in nature!... A Virgin Mary of the body!... And straightness!... It's a perfect straight line...like an illustration out of a plane geometry textbook.... And joints.... (*Quickly flips over a few more pictures. The images flash in front of the surgery candidate's eyes so fast he can't tell what they are like buildings close up to a railroad track seen from a fast-moving train. The doctor stops at a smaller picture, a 3 x 5, with two finger bones coming together in a joint.*) What beauty! Huh? (*Doesn't seem any longer to be speaking to the surgery candidate but to himself.*) Look at the delicate carving.... Like the head of an exquisitely carved violin...eighteenth-century Italian...a Stradivarius or a Guarnieri.... A marvel!... (*Stops looking down at the picture, speaks in abstract terms.*) The human body is a marvel...a marvel of engineering and art...functionality and beauty.... (*Stops. Without any warning goes to the bottom of the stack and extracts a picture showing the face of a woman in her thirties—white, strangely contorted like a muscle in a terrible, painful cramp, with only her right eye showing, protruding out of her face like an underdeveloped horn.*) And this.... Look.... A woman in agony...death throes...seconds before dying.... Her face already two-dimensional...a plane... belonging in a two-dimensional world...not ours.... Only her eye still struggling on...to stay behind...to be the last part of her to go...to stay alive...holding onto our three-dimensional world...objects...with the thin threads of her eyesight...until they break...one by one...as they always do....

The surgery candidate is speechless. He is standing on top of a very tall mountain and his breath has been knocked out of him by the vista below.

8. second second opinion

The surgery candidate's dream.

He is in the second opinion doctor's office in front of the cabinet with records in and on top of it. The stepladder already stands before him and he is about to climb it. He is to get up on top of the cabinet. He climbs the stepladder, lifts himself up on his arms onto the edge of the cabinet, and then brings up his feet. The cabinet is bigger in the dream than in reality—huge, like a stove in an old European peasant's home on top of which people sleep. It is cozy there and dark as it would be on top of such a stove and warm—a regular little room with a very low ceiling. He has to bend his head down as he is standing up on his knees. It seems in fact it is not a cabinet he is on top of but a stove. It is warm there and warmth is seeping up from the surface he is kneeling on into his knees.

There is a mattress—a thin pallet really—under his knees in fact and he is supposed to sleep there. But the doctor is standing at the foot of the stove/cabinet down below and is going to join him. He will have to help the man climb up because of the latter's artificial leg. But there isn't enough space for both of them to lie down so he has to make more room. Sacks filled with something are piled up high almost to the ceiling and he has to move them. There is room for them in the corner on his left so he starts moving them there. They are very light and crackle as he handles them and seem to be filled with dried long-stemmed plants. From touching them through the sacking they appear to be dried up gladioli. The doctor for some reason collects them.

Finally he has made enough room for both of them to lie down and he moves over to the edge of the stove (it is definitely a stove now) to help the doctor. He reaches down with his hand, the doctor climbs up the stepladder, stands on top of it, grabs the edge of the stove, lifts himself up on his arms—he helps him do this and then to bring his legs up, especially the artificial leg—and finally the doctor is sitting next to him. He has arranged his artificial leg to lie parallel to his good one and is breathing heavily through his nose. It was a big chore for him since he is so old and a cripple to boot. He (the surgery candidate) finds the sound the doctor is making pleasant though—soothing, as he recalls he found the sound of his father breathing next to him when he was little and the latter used to lie down beside him to tell him stories while putting him to sleep. The doctor's shoulder touches his and he feels warmth streaming from it into his body the same as from the stove underneath.

The doctor lies down and he is about to do the same but there still isn't enough room for him to be comfortable. He has to move more of the sacks over into the corner. He looks to his left toward the wall and sees there is only one sack there. It is much bigger than the other sacks were—longer and broader—like a mummy wrapped in a shroud. It seems in fact to be a shroud rather than a sack the thing is in for you can see the way it is wrapped around although the cloth is rough like burlap.

He touches the object and it seems to be very light, much lighter than a mummy would be. There are thin long things in it somewhat like the stalks of the dried flowers in the sacks he had put away earlier and he wonders if this is what they are again. But he is sure they are not that—they feel completely different. He would like to unwrap the object and to his delight notices the shroud isn't wrapped tightly around the body but loosely and haphazardly. It wouldn't be difficult for him to look under it.

He gets up on his knees again and starts unwrapping the object—pushing the cloth aside. It opens up very easily and soon he can look under it. It is a skeleton that lies wrapped in it! It must be a spare one the doctor has and he put it up there for lack of a better place. He wants to see the skeleton better, unwraps it more, and sees it's a skull with the empty eye sockets and the grinning teeth and then the bulging empty ribcage like a birdcage no longer used and the arms extended peacefully, parallel to the spine. The sight is perfectly pleasant, actually pacifying. He remembers he has to lie down too, so he starts covering up the skeleton to be able to do this. He covers it up carelessly however, just draping the sacking over it since there is no reason why it has to be carefully wrapped, and then turns the bundle on its side to make more room for himself.

Having done this he turns away and sits down preparing himself to stretch out. The doctor is on his right and he looks at him. The man lies dutifully stretched out like a soldier standing at attention but looks different than before. He is very thin under his clothes with arms and legs like broomsticks and his stomach sunken in like an old grave. Surprised but not shocked he (the surgery candidate) looks at the man's face and sees it is completely dried out too with the cheeks sunken in, eyelids flat and shiny with salt-like stuff coming out from under them, the lips pulled back and huge yellow teeth sticking out from between them in a sarcastic grin.

The sight doesn't surprise or shock him again however and he lies down and stretches himself out along the doctor's body on his right and the skeleton on his left. He can feel them through his clothes still and hard. He looks straight up and sees the ceiling very close above him. It is dark and when he closes his eyes there is no difference.

9. at the psychiatrist's

The surgery candidate at his psychiatrist's, early Saturday morning, one of two weekly sessions he has done regularly for the past five years (the other one being on Wednesday afternoons). He in an armchair with thin wooden arms, its back against the wall, the psychiatrist in the far corner on the left, comfortable in his overstuffed red imitation leather recliner, a couch matching the surgery candidate's armchair against the wall on the psychiatrist's right and the surgery candidate's left. The room dimly lit with an overhead light. Closed white venetian blinds on the window straight ahead of the surgery candidate with the shadow of a tree branch visible on them, delicate like a blooming plum tree branch in a Japanese painting. The shadow seeming to have a faint purplish tinge because of that.

The surgery candidate (*continuing; the conversation was started by his remarking on the shadow of the tree branch on the venetian blind*): I don't know what's going to happen if it doesn't start raining soon.

The psychiatrist (*in his heavily accented Scottish accent*): It won't! You can bet your bottom dollar on it! It's been nine months now and I think we're in for a long haul.

The surgery candidate (*concerned*): You really think so?

The psychiatrist: No doubt about it!... Statistics tell you that.... The longer a phenomenon lasts the more chance it has of lasting.

The surgery candidate (*after deliberating for a moment*): This would mean that the longer you live the longer you're likely to stay alive, which would mean old people have a better chance of living than the young and ultimately that there's a chance of some people living forever....

The psychiatrist (*laughing heartily*): Oh, you don't understand statistics. Older people do in fact have a better chance of living longer than young ones. If life expectancy of males in a society is seventy-five, then a seventy-four-year-old man has a better chance of living till seventy-five than a thirty-year-old one. And a seventy-five-year-old man has a hundred percent probability—certainty—of being seventy-five. But his chances of being a hundred aren't one hundred and aren't as high as those of a thirty-year-old man being seventy-five. And everyone's chances of being two hundred are zero because no one has lived that long.

The surgery candidate (*gives up on the topic which he doesn't know much about and goes back to the original subject*): It's only April and look at how bad things are. I dread to think what it's going to be like in the summer....

The psychiatrist: Two years ago we had a dry spell and we started having forest fires. That was a preview of things to come. I think the climate's changing.... You and I will probably never see those stretches of rainy weather again. Our life might change drastically.... It's probably due to global warming.

The surgery candidate: Yes.... They've outlawed car washing and have restrictions on watering lawns.... Every other day a couple of hours in the morning and at night....

The psychiatrist: That's nothing.... More severe restrictions might come.... Water to the public just a couple of hours a day...restrictions on industry...closing some businesses.... Many countries do it already.... We've been lucky...and profligate.... We have to change our ways.

The surgery candidate (*doesn't know what to say*): Yeah....

Silence follows. The surgery candidate realizes the subject has been exhausted but can't think of another one. Feels uncomfortable, on the spot. Knows he should come up with something. His mind squirms as if in a hot skillet. He then notices a subject that has been pestering him constantly—his recent obsession with gladioli. The discussion about the drought may have brought it to the surface—plants and water. He realizes he saw them in the office of the surgeon he had consulted but that doesn't explain the feeling he has for them—he loves them. Decides to talk about this to the psychiatrist.

The surgery candidate: I've had this image of gladioli on my mind lately.... Can't figure out why.

The psychiatrist: "Gladioli?" I thought it was "gladioluses."

The surgery candidate (*uneasiness all gone; all excited; etymology is one of his passions*): It could be "gladioluses" but also "gladiola...." Or even "gladiolus"—the plural the same as the singular. But "gladioli" appears to be the preferred form, pehaps because people have become more urbane, more educated...want to show off that they know or have heard of Latin.... Nouns ending in "*us*" end in "*i*" in the plural.... For instance "*lupus/ lupi.*" Anyway, why should I like them?

The psychiatrist: Have you always liked them?

The surgery candidate (*thinks, then speaks reluctantly*): Yes, sort of, but not to the same degree. They're on my mind all the time.

The psychiatrist: What do they make you think of? What do you associate them with?

The surgery candidate: (*thinks again, then answers even more reluctantly*): Birds, I think...geese, swans....

The psychiatrist: In what way?

The surgery candidate: (*hesitates as before*): I don't know.... They're shaped like birds...necks, beaks...

The psychiatrist: Beaks? Their flowers are feathery, like irises. Is it the feathers?

The surgery candidate (*surprised*): Feathers? No. You're right. Their flowers are more like irises.... In fact, I think they are kind of an iris.... I think I've been thinking of birds of paradise. Gladioluses, I mean gladioli, make me think of birds of paradise, so that's probably why I think of geese and swans...white gladioli.... But I don't think that's the reason I like them.... At least not the only reason. (*Thinks on, then speaks, excited.*) Wait a minute.... "Gladiolus" and "gladiator" are related. They come from the same Latin word—*"gladius,"* meaning "sword." "Gladiator" is someone who wields a sword and "gladiolus" is a small sword, a "swordlet...." (*Ponders, then speaks as if to himself.*) But it's soft, so it's a soft sword.... That's interesting.... I guess I'd like swords to be soft....

10. the mountain

The surgery candidate's dream.

He is with his wife and they are climbing a mountain. He has asked her to buy a mountain with the half of their estate that is rightfully his when he dies and to dedicate it to his memory. It is this mountain she will buy. Actually she seems to have bought it already because he feels the mountain is his.

The mountain isn't very steep—barely a gentle incline—and there are other people going along with him and his wife as if on a picnic or in a pilgrimage to a shrine. There are trees all around as in a forest and people can be seen sitting on the ground picnicking. They have stopped to rest before continuing to climb to the top. It isn't daytime but neither is it night. The light is diffused as if at early dawn or late dusk.

It must be in the summer, for people are lightly dressed. The atmosphere is cheerful. People are chatting and laughing as they briskly walk along.

Eventually he and his wife have arrived where they were going. In the clearing among the trees there is a small hillock and he will climb to the top of it. It is bare of trees, with only sparse grass growing on it, and seems to be man-made. The people that have been around him and his wife stop, as does his wife, and he quickly runs to the top of the hillock. It is perhaps ten feet tall.

He feels joyful to be standing on top of the hillock, proud the mountain is his, and he turns around to see the people that have gathered around him. They cheer him on and wave their arms and he waves back to them, smiling. The crowd that has gathered is fairly big and in it he sees some familiar faces, members of his family, friends, and coworkers, as well as his wife. She stands in the front row and waves and cheers him on most enthusiastically as is to be expected.

Suddenly he feels unsteady on his feet—it is as if he were about to lose his balance. He looks down and sees the hillock has shrunk to a small mound of earth under him. He tries to stand on top of it and has a hard time keeping his feet together. They keep slipping off the mound as if he were standing on top of a bowling ball.

He spreads his arms out to help himself balance and at first this helps but then he feels unsteady again. The mound under his feet has shrunk more. He tells himself he has to try harder not to fall but it is of no use. The mound continues shrinking, gets to be the size of a tennis ball, and he falls.

It is pitch-dark. Everybody is gone.

11. the belly of the shadow

Night. The bedroom dark, almost not there, except the eight (two visible) corners deforming the darkness like mass deforming space, according to Einstein, stretching it out until it breaks. The surgery candidate and his wife in bed, both on their left sides, he behind her, his body dovetailing perfectly with her S-shaped form like a piece of ivory carefully cut out to be inlaid in a slot in wood. Her warmth seeping into him along the top of his thighs, belly, midriff, and chest. His right arm draped over her body, the hand probing the warm, yielding abdomen.

The surgery candidate (*continuing*): Are you sure?

The surgery candidate's wife (*half-asleep, from under the blanket*): Uh-huh.

The surgery candidate (*after a deep sigh and a few seconds' silence*): It's at times like these that a pretty *au-pair* girl would come in handy.

The surgery candidate's wife (*after a few seconds' silence*): Uh-huh.

The surgery candidate (*probing*): From Italy...named Beatrice... (*after a pause*) or Holland...Beatrix.

No sound from the surgery candidate's wife. The surgery candidate gropes around with his hand in the softness of her abdomen as if in darkness.

The surgery candidate (*when it is clear she will not speak*): You agree?

The surgery candidate's wife: Uh-huh.

The surgery candidate (*incredulous*): Are you sure?

The surgery candidate's wife: Uh-huh.

The surgery candidate: You won't be jealous?

The surgery candidate's wife: Uh-huh.

The surgery candidate (*more incredulous*): Are you sure?

The surgery candidate's wife: Uh-huh.

The surgery candidate would like to continue the topic but feels it is exhausted. Is disappointed. Doesn't know what to say. Becomes aware of his right hand on his wife's abdomen. The latter's softness for the first time makes him think of darkness. The word "tenebrousness" comes up in his mind. He wonders if such a word exists. Knows that "tenebrous" is an English word and concludes that "tenebrousness" should be too, although it might not have been officially attested. But is sure someone must have used it. Drops the subject. Moves his hand over his wife's abdomen and imagines it being a person moving lost through semidarkness. Thinks of Poe's poem "Eldorado," about the knight journeying "in shadow." Thinks of the person as himself. Notices another association rising up in his mind but it doesn't quite make it to the surface. He is left only with the words "valley" and "shadow." Drops the subject. Imagines steep walls rising on both his sides as in a ravine. There is darkness up ahead and behind and steep unscalable walls on the right and left. He moves his fingers along his wife's abdomen to imitate walking, thinking of the ad for Yellow Pages that says "Let your fingers do the walking."

The surgery candidate's wife (*wiggling her abdomen under her fingers, trying to move away; in a clear voice*): Stop tickling me!

The surgery candidate (*continuing to move his fingers*): I'm not tickling you, I'm walking….

The surgery candidate's wife (*angry, threatening to move away for good*): Stop it!

The surgery candidate makes his fingers stop. Gives a deep sigh. Leaves his hand where it is, however. It hangs limp over the soft abdomen. He wants to say something to his wife about whether she will always stay with him but decides against it. Thinks it is pointless.

12. what do flowers tell the poet about life?

After Rimbaud

the poor depressed perhaps lame
poet thinking he is just
strolling but in need of urgent spirit
ual support in reality takes
a stroll through the

early gloomy Sunday

morning streets purged of life

traffic his body weighing heavily on

his mind soul keeps

hoping to see a tall gray

stone facade rising triumphant

ly toward a tall gray stone

spire rising triumph

antly toward the low gray

stone sky a church

portal with a door in

it he could pass

through is passing through a

run-down neighbor

hood garbage on the

sidewalks run-down abandoned

buildings vacant

lots on both sides of the

street sees a vacant

lot narrow space between

two narrow abandoned

buildings with broken

windows boarded up with

plywood left over from a

building recently razed sees

the gray sky above

it at its end suddenly has a

vision a tall gray stone

facade at the top of the stairs high
above the sidewalk a yellow
varnished oak door in it it
opens a slender tall female
figure steps out from the
opening all dressed
in white veil full length wedding
dress shoes teeth like a posy of lilies
of the valley between the parted
lips a huge bundle of white
flowers in her arms lilies?
gladioli? all flowers roses peonies
jonquils colors of all
flowers red blue yellow merged into
white they carry
her not she them the
door opens wide the two
wings fly out a mass
of flowers pushes its
way out into the world the
doorway creaks tears like the
corners of a mouth an a
nus a beautiful vomiting a
defecation of constipated
beauty natural or
ganic the solid current
spills over the stairs the
girl woman (has just gotten

married) has disap

peared in it become

part of it the poet

is caught by its gears

flowers too carried along into

the street the vast current

river turns left flows

down it toward the distant

horizon the street is filled with

it side to side ground to

the tops of the buildings it

picks up everything it

comes across shopping

carts cars refrigerators

washing machines radios T

V sets people they bob up

and down in it eight-year-old

boys girls in white on their

way to first communions holding lit

candles guarding white petal

flames surgeons nurses in old-fashioned

white outfits bakers their

clothes faces dusted with

flour butchers in crisp white

starched aprons undertakers in white

tuxedos the river moves along now

spilled from distant horizon to distant

horizon the poet's head

bobs up and down in it his face

smiling white hand reaching

for or already clutching a

blank white page

13. to the hospital

"...Tower of Paine*," thinks the surgery candidate, the image of a vertical wall of sheer rock going straight up into a white sky above him flashing in his mind. "Tower of pain," he thinks on, one corner of his mouth creasing itself in what eventually would be a smile. He stops his mouth from misbehaving however and goes back to reality.

He stands under the awning of a flower shop/grocery store on the corner of two streets, stopped there by a sudden downpour of a heavy April shower on his way to the hospital where he is to undergo surgery. He is dressed in a mountain climbing/hiking outfit, mostly yellow, consisting of heavy canvas-topped boots, ribbed knee-high socks, knickers, sweater with a parka over it, and a wool cap, and carries a rucksack on his back with a loop of rope and a bunch of pitons held together like a cluster of grapes on the outside. In his hand he is holding a long-handled mountain climber's pickax, which he has been using as a cane.

---

* Torres del Paine (pronounced "PIE-neh")—Three tall mountains, towers of sheer rock going straight up, in Chilean Patagonia.

The rain is heavy, and thick long tassels of water constantly appear and disappear on the edge of the awning. The latter is green and white striped with a low overhang. The surgery candidate is hoping for the rain to stop soon so that he can continue on his way. He doesn't have very much time left and still has quite a way to go. He has been periodically glancing with concern at his wristwatch.

The surgery candidate has labeled in his mind the store as a flower shop/grocery store because under the awning there is a huge stock of flowers arranged in multicolored rows on the gradually ascending shelves that look like bleachers, and people have been going out of the store with bags of groceries containing loaves of bread, packaged and canned goods, and bottles of soda, juice, and beer. The place seems to be doing a booming business in both areas. There is no attendant under the awning by the flowers but there must be someone responsible for them inside. The surgery candidate was the only one under the awning when he came there but with the rain continuing another half a dozen people have collected around him waiting for the rain to stop as he does.

The flower shop/grocery store is on the corner of two streets and the awning wraps around it, which reminds the surgery candidate of scenes from France—Paris—in pictures in textbooks on French he has seen in his many superficial attempts at learning that language. He has not seen many such setups in America.

When this realization forms itself in the surgery candidate's mind, as if on command, the scene starts changing from that

of a present day modern American city to France—Paris
again—in the forties and fifties. The traffic gets sparser and
there are more older cars, European-looking to boot, and people come strolling by dressed in hooded rubber jackets leading
old-fashioned bicycles by their handles as if placid oxen by
their silver horns. ("Where have I read this phrase?" wonders
the surgery candidate referring to the last simile. He can't find
an answer to his question.)

Then an old beat-up truck appears from somewhere, stops
across the street, men in dark blue overalls and knee-high rubber boots with black berets on their heads get out of it and
start unloading bricks which they stack up against the side of
the building on the opposite corner. Apparently some construction project is in progress/about to start there. The street
is narrow (the smaller of the two—a side street) and the surgery candidate is able to hear the men talk. To his surprise they
speak French.

The surgery candidate is puzzled by this but accepts it as reality—all sorts of unexpected things happen in life. The common thing about life is its uncommonness.

There are lots of bricks in the truck and the men go on working in the rain as if nothing were happening, not complaining
about getting drenched, and the pile grows slowly—square and
neat against the dirty beat-up wall of the building. The rain
keeps coming down heavy, the tassels of water form and fall
off the edge of the awning, the people in hooded rubber jackets keep on leading their obedient bicycles someplace (virtually
all of them walk in the same direction), and the sparse traffic

in the main street goes by, each vehicle a ball of darkness enveloped by mist and of a whooshing sound.

The flowers are long rows of vivid colors—reds, blues, yellows, whites, etc., arranged along the ascending shelves. The surgery candidate looks at them to give his eyes a rest from the monochrome monotony of the two streets, and identifies among the flowers roses, tulips, orchids, asters, daisies, lilies of the valley, and finally, his favorites, gladioli—red, pink, salmon-colored, and (his favorite again) white. He likes these flowers for their size and sturdiness and they make him think of living creatures that could make it on their own.

Suddenly he realizes they make him think of long-necked and long-beaked birds—storks and cranes—and then that when the men across the street finish unloading bricks the necks of these birds, already dead, will appear hanging limply draped over the edge of the end of the truck.

The image is highly unpleasant to the surgery candidate and he tries to get rid of it by a mental process similar to gulping. That doesn't help however and he turns away from the truck to face the main street. The chatter of the men irritates him however and he thinks: "Damn Frogs…. Where did they come from?" They must be Quebecois, he concludes, rather than French. Perhaps they brought the load of bricks all the way from Canada. The latter look different than the bricks he is used to.

The rain continues unabated. The tassels of water on the edge of the awning appear and disappear with greater frequency. The street is a river now with the vehicles in it fording it in the direction of its flow having lost their way in the mist. They will never make it to the other side! The surgery candidate remembers the hospital and the fact he is expected there. His heart sinks. He looks at his wristwatch and realizes he will have to brave the rain.